The Case of the Blazing Sky

The Case of the Blazing Sky

John R. Erickson

Illustrations by Gerald L. Holmes

Viking

VIKING
Published by Penguin Group
Penguin Young Readers Group, 345 Hudson Street, New York, New York 10014, U.S.A.
Penguin Group (Canada), 90 Eglinton Avenue East, Suite 700, Toronto,
Ontario, Canada M4P 2Y3 (a division of Pearson Penguin Canada Inc.)
Penguin Books Ltd, 80 Strand, London WC2R 0RL, England
Penguin Ireland, 25 St Stephen's Green, Dublin 2, Ireland
(a division of Penguin Books Ltd)
Penguin Group (Australia), 250 Camberwell Road, Camberwell,
Victoria 3124, Australia (a division of Pearson Australia Group Pty Ltd)
Penguin Books India Pvt Ltd, 11 Community Centre,
Panchsheel Park, New Delhi - 110 017, India
Penguin Group (NZ), 67 Apollo Drive, Rosedale, North Shore 0632, New Zealand
(a division of Pearson New Zealand Ltd)
Penguin Books (South Africa) (Pty) Ltd, 24 Sturdee Avenue,
Rosebank, Johannesburg 2196, South Africa

Registered Offices: Penguin Books Ltd, 80 Strand, London WC2R 0RL, England

Published simultaneously in the United States of America by Viking
Children's Books and Puffin Books, divisions of Penguin Young Readers Group, 2008

1   3   5   7   9   10   8   6   4   2

LIBRARY OF CONGRESS CATALOGING-IN-PUBLICATION DATA
Erickson, John R., date-
The case of the blazing sky / by John R. Erickson ; illustrations by
Gerald L. Holmes.
p. cm.—(Hank the Cowdog ; 51)
Summary: With the threat of prairie fires looming, security expert
Hank the Cowdog takes on extra duties as Head of Fire Safety, while
trying to resist the mouth-watering hens in Sally May's chicken house.
ISBN 978-0-14-241015-8 (pbk.)—ISBN 978-0-670-06260-7 (hardcover)
[1. Dogs—Fiction. 2. Ranch life—Texas—Fiction. 3. Fires—Fiction.
4.Texas—Fiction. 5. Humorous stories.] I. Holmes, Gerald L., ill. II. Title.
PZ7.E72556Cacb 2008   [Fic]—dc22   2007033630

Hank the Cowdog® is a registered trademark of John R. Erickson.
Printed in the United States of America

To a whole bunch of Rinkers
who live in Perryton

CONTENTS

The Case of the Blazing Sky

CHAPTER ONE

We Discover
a Hooded Monster

It's me again, Hank the Cowdog. Maybe I haven't mentioned this before, but I'm not only Head of Ranch Security but also Chief of our ranch's fire department. That's an important piece of information because this story has a lot to do with fires and firefighting.

It's pretty impressive that a dog can go from being an ace crimefighter to being an ace firefighter, and move elephantly from one area of expertise to the other.

Wait. Did I say elephantly? I meant *elegantly*. To move elephantly would suggest that I'm clumsy and awkward, and nothing could be farther from the truth. There is nothing elephantly

1

about the way I move from one job to another. Sorry for the confusion.

Fighting fires would be a HUGE deal for most of your ordinary mutts. Show 'em a raging prairie fire and they'll hide under the nearest pickup, but that's not the way we operate around here. Show us a fire and we whip the stuffing out of it.

Anyway, the point is that this story will have a lot of scary stuff about fires. It will have quite a bit about chickens, too, but that's a touchy subject and I'd rather not discuss it just yet. For now, let's not say a word about chickens.

Okay, maybe I'll say just a few words. Nothing in this world has caused me more grief than Sally May's flock of idiot birds. I have the job of protecting them, don't you see, and sometimes it drives me to despair. They are so dumb! But the most challenging part of protecting our chickens from villains who love to eat them is that every once in a while, a guard dog finds himself . . . slurp.

Never mind. I said we wouldn't discuss this sensitive subject and, by George, we won't. Talking about chickens is not only a teetotal waste of time, but I've also noticed that whenever chickens enter the conversation, I'm usually . . . well, in trouble.

Hencely, I won't say one word about chickens,

even though I already did, and I'd be grateful if you'd forget about it. I said nothing about chickens, right? Thanks.

Where were we? Oh yes, it was the month of September and I don't remember the year. It was the year we had September between August and October. August had been wet and cool, and our pastures had turned into a grass paradise. We had water flowing in the creek and standing in every hole and cow track. The cows and yearlings were fat and some local fools (Slim and Loper, for example) had ventured the opinion that we would have green grass all the way to frost. Ha.

Then came September with temperatures up near a hundred degrees and those hot southwest winds that steal moisture like a thief. Within two weeks, our country changed from green to brown, and the mood of everyone on the ranch went into a steep decline.

Me? I didn't have time to feel gloomy about the dry weather, because someone on the ranch had to worry about the danger of fires. Yes sir. When you get that combination of tall dry grass and hot southwest winds, you have all the ingredients for a disastrous prairie fire.

Those fires get started in many ways: a careless camper, a cigarette tossed out the window of a passing vehicle, a lightning strike, a power line that has been blown down in the wind.

Oh, and let's not forget sparks that come from electric welders and cutting torches. When the country is dry and windblown, only a moron would try to cut and weld steel, but you know what? *It happens.* And you know what else? It happened on my own ranch, before my very eyes, and, as you will see, it almost burned the pants off the guy who did it.

It was Drover who turned in the report of suspicious activity. It was a blistery hot afternoon and we were occupying a piece of shade on the north side of the saddle shed. I had been logging eighteen hours a day on Fire Patrol and was worn out from all the stress and strain, and I had seized the opportunity to . . . well, grab a few winks of sleep.

"Hank, you'd better look at this. Something's going on."

I lifted my head and glared at him through soggy eyes. "Drover, something is always going on. At any moment, in any part of the universe, something will be going on."

"Yeah, but you won't like this. Someone's down at the corrals, and I think he's running a welder."

It was then that my ears picked up the drone

of a portable welder's gasoline engine. I shifted my gaze to the northwest and focused in on the scene. Sure enough, some guy was down there, welding the cow chute.

As you may know, a cow chute is a device that is used to restrain cattle, so that the cowboy crew can perform medical services that cows don't necessarily want to receive. The chute is made of steel bars. When a cow walks into it, the cowboys trap her head in the "head gate" and compress the sides, holding her in one place whilst they give her a shot, check her temperature, or doctor an infected wound.

A cow chute is a handy piece of equipment, but thousand-pound animals take their toll, even on steel, and from time to time, our lads have to crank up the welder and do some repairs. But in the middle of a dry spell? That was a no-no.

"I don't believe this, Drover. I was up all night, scouting for fires, and here's some nut running a welder in the heat of the day! Why, he could start a fire that would burn this whole ranch to the ground."

"Yeah, I wonder who it could be?"

I leaped to my feet and loosened up the enormous muscles in my shoulders. "Nobody on our ranch would do such a crazy thing. He must be a stranger. Let's go to Code Three and put a stop to this nonsense."

We went streaking through the corrals, ducking under gates and bottom boards of the corral fence, and arrived at the scene only minutes later. There before us, we saw a strange man, working under a welding hood and creating a shower of red and yellow sparks.

In the corral, there wasn't much vegetation that could burn, just a small patch of weeds at his feet, so maybe the fire danger wasn't all that great, but operating a welder during a drought was against regulations. And this guy needed a good scolding.

I studied his appearance and memorized even the tiniest of details. He was fairly tall and thin, wearing steel-toed lace-up work boots and a pair of blue coveralls that were spotted with grease. Little burned holes on the sleeves suggested that the guy often used these coveralls as his welding uniform.

Oh, and did I mention the ragged cuffs? The cuffs around both ankles were frayed into strings.

It was those ragged cuffs that helped me identify the culprit. I had seen them before. "Drover, I've got him identified. You know who that is? Slim Chance."

Drover was as shocked as I was. "No fooling? But why . . ."

"We don't have an answer to that, son, but he should know better than to run a welder in the middle of a drought. Oh, and don't look at the fire."

"Okay. What fire?"

"The flash of the welder. It will blister your eyes."

"I'll be derned. How can it blister your eyes?"

"Drover, we don't know all the details, but I've heard the cowboys tell Little Alfred not to look into the flash of an arc welder. It can blister the eyes. That's why men who are welding wear hoods, to protect their eyes."

"I wondered about that. He looks kind of like a robot, doesn't he?"

"No. He looks like a man welding."

"Well, I remember the time you barked at him, 'cause you thought he was a robot monster. I saw it myself."

I heaved a sigh. "Drover, that was long ago. Many bridges have gone underwater since then."

"Well, he still looks like a robot to me."

"He's *not* a robot and please hush. Stand by, I'm fixing to give him a wake-up call." I stepped forward and delivered a stern round of barking that said, "Hey, pal, did you happen to notice the dead weeds at your feet? You're violating the Fire Code. Shut off the welder and find something else to do."

Heh heh. That got his attention. He stopped welding and turned toward the sound of my barking. He looked at me with . . . hmmm, he seemed to be staring at me through that one slit-eye on the front of the welding hood.

Behind me, I heard Drover gasp. "Oh my gosh, look at that creepy eye!"

"Drover, please hush. All welding hoods have a slit of dark glass that—"

Huh? You won't believe this. Even I couldn't believe it. All at once the man in the welding suit raised a clawed hand in the air and we heard this . . . this deep mysterious GROWL coming from inside the hood.

Drover began backing away. "Oh my gosh, I knew it! Did you hear that? He's growling at us! And look at those claws!"

"Drover, hold your position and quit—"

"GRRRRRRRRRRRR! ROWERRRRRR! GR-RRRRR!"

Holy smokes, something horrible was taking place! I mean, we'd been sitting there, minding our own business and watching a guy do some

repairs on a cow chute, right? Well, get this. Before our very eyes, the man we'd always known as Slim Chance was somehow transformed into a . . . into a huge *robot monster*, eight feet tall!

Hang on, it gets worse. This huge monster saw us sitting there and he started slouching toward us with deadly claws poised above his head. And all at once it became perfectly clear that . . . HE ATE DOGS!

Well, you know me. I'm no prisoner to past memories. Maybe that guy had once been my friend, but by George, something awful had happened to him and now . . .

My ears flew up on my head, my eyes popped wide open, and the hair stood up on the back of my neck. I took a step backward and summoned up the best bark I could muster on short notice. Okay, it was kind of a gurgle, but what's a guy to do when he suddenly realizes that one of his very best friends has been monsterized?

What had happened to poor Slim? We didn't know. Maybe he had stared into the flash of the welder and it had . . . I don't know, boiled his chromatoids and changed him into a slouching monster robot.

Science doesn't have an answer for every question. All we know for certain is that this is a very strange world we live in and . . . yipes! He took another step in my direction and, fellers, I didn't wait around for science to figure this one out. I whirled around, pushed the throttle up to Turbo Six, and hauled the mail out of there, firing barks over my shoulder as I—

BAM!

Ran into the fence. But that was only a momentary distraction. I leaped to my feet and roared away like a greased lightning bug.

If that creature planned to eat me, he would have to start with the tail and work his way up.

ZOOM!

CHAPTER TWO

The Lost
Mackerel

I didn't slow down until I had reached the saddle shed. Whew! Boy, that was close. There, I stopped for a breath of air and found Drover hiding in some weeds nearby. He was shaking all over and his eyes had turned into plates.

"I told you he was a robot monster!"

"Drover, you said he *might* be a robot, but you said nothing about a monster."

"No, I said he was both and you didn't listen. You never listen."

"Okay, maybe I didn't listen and maybe you were right this time. I'm sorry."

"Are you really sorry or just saying it to be nice?"

I gave the runt a scorching glare. "Look, pal, we survived. You don't get a medal for being right once every five years."

"Yeah, but he could have eaten us for supper."

"He didn't eat us for supper. We're alive and I've admitted that I underestimated the crisis. What more do you want?"

"I want to go home!"

"You are home. This ranch is where you live."

He blinked his eyes and glanced around. "I guess you're right, but I don't feel any better. What'll we do now?"

"I'm not sure. It's pretty clear that we've lost Slim."

"Poor old Slim! I really liked the guy. He used to let us sleep inside the house on cold nights."

"I know, and he was always willing to share his ketchup and mackerel sandwiches."

Drover gave his head a sad shake. "Yeah, they always made me sick, but he tried to be a friend."

"Yes, those were the worst sandwiches I ever ate. I never understood why he kept eating canned mackerel."

"Cheap."

I glanced around. "Did you hear that?"

"What?"

"I think it was a bird. It said 'cheep.'"

"No, it was—"

"Quiet. I'd better check this out."

"Yeah, but—"

"Shhhh!" I rose to my feet and studied the treetops in the tops of all the nearby trees. "That bird made an unusual sound, almost like the call of a . . . well, a young chicken in distress." Suddenly and mysteriously, I felt a rush of water in my mouth. "A tender, juicy young . . . slurp . . . chicken."

"Hank, is your mouth watering?"

"Uh . . . yes, but how did you know that?"

"Well, I heard you licking your chops."

I cut my eyes from side to side and a cunning smile worked its way across my dripping mouth. "You know, Drover, this could turn out to be . . . uh . . . very interesting. A poor youthful chicken has wandered away from the chicken house and lost its way. One of our jobs on this ranch is to . . . well, to supervise, so to speak, the comings and goings of Sally May's chickens, right?"

"Yeah, but . . ."

"And if a chicken has lost its way, the Security Division must swing into action."

Drover let out a moan. "Hank, I don't like that look in your eyes. It makes me think . . ."

I lumbered over to him. "My eyes have nothing

to do with it. Let me go straight to the point. Are you hungry?"

"Well . . . I guess so."

"Are you aware that our dog food bowl was empty this morning?"

"Yeah, I guess Slim forgot to fill it."

"There you are. After all the work we do for this ranch, don't we deserve a decent meal?"

He stared at me. "You mean, eat one of—"

I covered his mouth with a paw. "Hush, don't say it out loud! Someone might be listening."

"Muff muff murff."

"What? Speak up." I noticed that my paw was covering his mouth. I removed it. "Oh. Sorry. What were you saying?"

"I said, that 'cheap' you heard wasn't a chicken. It was me."

"What I heard was a chicken."

"No, it was me, honest."

I stuck my nose in his face and raised my voice. "Drover, don't tell me what I heard. Am I chopped liver or the Head of Ranch Security?"

"Well . . ."

"I'm Head of Ranch Security and I know the sound of a chicken. What I heard was a chicken."

"No, we were talking about mackerel sandwiches, remember?"

"Are you saying that I heard a mackerel?"

"No, you wondered how come Slim eats . . . you said . . . I said . . ." He collapsed on the ground and started crying. "I don't know what I said! I can't think when you're yelling at me."

I gave him a moment to sniffle his way through the crisis. "Drover, I think I can wrap this up, but you have to stop blubbering."

"I'm not blubbering."

"You're blubbering. Now get control of yourself and listen." He sat up and brushed the tears out of his eyes. "I've decided that you were right."

"No fooling?"

"Yes. The sound we heard was not a chicken. It came from a mackerel, a lost mackerel. I'm going in search of the mackerel and you're going to stay here."

He stared at me. "How come I have to stay here?"

"Because, Drover, you're not old enough for this kind of work. It might be dangerous."

He narrowed his eyes. "I get it now. You're going to catch a chicken, aren't you?"

I turned away from him before he could see . . . slurp . . . that the very word *chicken* had caused my mouth to start watering again. "I'm slurped that you would even think such a thing."

17

"Yeah, but it's true, isn't it?"

"Absolutely not. What kind of dog do you think I am?"

"Hungry . . . and maybe crazy enough to eat a chicken."

"Okay, buddy, that did it! Go to your room and stick your nose in the corner for one hour."

"One hour! How come?"

"Go! I'll be watching, so don't try to cheat."

He whined and begged for mercy, but my heart had turned to stone. The very idea, the little mutt thinking that I might eat one of Sally May's slurpens . . . uh, chickens. If there was ever a dog who needed to stand with his nose in the corner, it was Drover.

He went to his room and I found myself all alone with my, uh, thoughts. To be honest, I was having some pretty wonderful thoughts about . . . well, you know, sunsets and rainbows and . . . okay, maybe food.

Dogs think about food, right? It's normal and healthy. You'd worry about a dog that didn't think about food every once in a while. Mackerel, that's what I was thinking about. No kidding.

I lifted my eyes and did another scan of the treetops. I saw no sign of the, uh, mackerel, the lost mackerel, shall we say, so I lowered my nose to the ground and began searching for tracks . . . mackerel tracks, of course.

You didn't know that mackerels leave tracks? Ha ha. Okay, maybe they don't, because they don't have feet or legs, and it's hard to leave tracks when you have no feet. But a guy never knows until he checks these things out.

I found no fish tracks, but the ground was covered with chicken tracks. Interesting. Perhaps if I followed the chicken tracks far enough, I would find . . . well, you know, a mackerel or something.

Remember the old saying? At the end of every rainbow is a pot of mackerel.

I put my nose to the groundstone and followed the line of tracks in a northerly direction. After sniffing my way through a grove of young chinaberry trees, I looked up and was surprised to find myself standing in front of the . . . well, in front of the chicken house.

Okay, maybe that wasn't exactly the biggest surprise of the year. I mean, if you follow a line of chicken tracks far enough, they'll lead you to the chicken house, so we'll cancel what I said about being surprised.

I wasn't exactly surprised. What I felt was . . . slurp . . . a sudden rush of water and digestive juices into my mouthalary region, and once again

I had to, uh, lick my chops to mop up the excess water.

It's funny, how that happens. The mouth of a dog seems to have a mind of its own, don't you see, and certain thoughts or mental pictures seem to set off the water business.

Hmmm. You know, I'm not sure we should be discussing this. I mean, all dogs have secret thoughts. I wouldn't want the little children to think that I . . . well, spent half my life dreaming about . . . slurp.

I mean, we're talking about the Head of Ranch Security, right? The Head of Ranch Security is charged with the responsibility of guarding Sally May's chickens against attacks by coyotes, skunks, raccoons, hawks, owls, and your various forms of Night Monster, and nobody would ever believe that we might consider . . . well, eating the very chickens we have sworn an oath to protect.

Slurp.

How absurd. You would never believe such a pack of lies, right? Thanks. I knew you wouldn't. These rumors are started by our enemies, you know. Yes. They scheme day and night on ways to weaken our security systems, planting their poisoned seeds that grow into . . . something. Poison oak trees, I suppose.

And speaking of schemers, speaking of letting the cat out of the sandbox, would you like to guess who showed up at the very moment that I was . . . well, at the very moment that I was absolutely no-way thinking about chicken dinners?

Mister Kitty Moocher. Mister Never Sweat. Mister Loaf in the Iris Patch. Pete the Barncat.

CHAPTER THREE

I Honk
the Cat

Have we discussed my Position on Cats? I don't like 'em, never have. As a group, they are lazy, selfish, arrogant, and generally worthless. And dumb, extremely dumb.

They don't have jobs, you know. They don't contribute anything to the good of the world, and they seem to think their whole purpose in life is to cause trouble. Oh, and to rub on anything that doesn't kick them away.

That's what he was doing . . . Pete, that is . . . sliding his way along the front of the machine shed, rubbing, purring, and wearing that insolent smirk that drives me nuts. The very sight of the little pest threw my entire body into a scramble of activity.

My ears shot up. My tail froze, and we're talking about stiff as a tree limb. The skin around my mouth began to twitch, like the fingers of a gunslinger reaching for his pistol. The hair on the back of my neck stood straight up and a growl began to rumble in the deep recesses of my throatalary region.

Any animal with an ounce of sense would have read the warning signs and vanished into the shadows. Not Pete. He saw nothing, missed the whole show, and here he came. After rubbing all the paint off the side of the machine shed, he slithered across the gravel drive, came over to me, and began rubbing on my front legs.

"Hi, Hankie."

I HATE the way he says that. He has this high-pitched, whiny tone of voice, don't you see, and I'm sure he spends hours and hours rehearsing it, so that every word he says will grate on my nerves.

"Get away from me, you little python! You know I can't stand you rubbing on my legs."

"Oh really! I didn't know that, Hankie."

"Of course you knew it; now get away from me."

Did he take the hint? Of course not. Cats don't take hints. Taking hints is a sign of intelligence and he had none of that. You know what he did? He not only continued to rub on my legs but also flicked his tail across my nose.

Okay, that did it! I sucked in a huge gulp of air and delivered a type of barking we call Train Horns: BWONK!

Heh heh. It's a special category of barking we use for waking up cats that are sleepwalking through life. Done properly, the Train Horns Program will not only part their hair but also send them rolling backward.

Heh heh. I got 'im good, blew him right out of his tracks and sent him rolling across the gravel drive, hissing and spitting. I loved it, absolutely loved it. I'm not sure I'd ever done a better job of Train Horns. Old Pete knew he'd been honked.

He picked himself off the ground and beamed me a sour look. "Now, why did you have to go and do that, Hankie? It seemed almost unfriendly."

"Yeah? Maybe you're getting the picture, kitty. It seemed unfriendly because it *was* unfriendly. Don't you get it? I don't like being used as a rubbing post. I don't like cats and, most of all, I don't like you. Is there anything else I need to explain?"

He gave that some thought. "Well, you seem a little vague, Hankie. Are you saying that you really don't like cats?"

"Right, yes. That's what I'm saying."

"And you'd rather that I didn't rub on your legs?"

"Exactly. Keep going."

"What are you doing up here, Hankie?"

"What?"

He was staring at me with those weird yellow eyes, tapping his paw on the ground and twitching the last two inches of his tail. "I asked what you're doing up here."

I shot a glance over my shoulder. All at once I had the feeling that I was . . . well, being watched. "Why do you ask?"

"Well, Hankie, cats are very perceptive, you know."

"Hurry up."

"And, well, I noticed a strange kind of light in your eyes, almost as though . . ."

I moved closer. "As though what? Get to the point."

He smirked and pointed his paw toward the west. "The chicken house is right over there, Hankie."

"Yes, and so what? It's been there for fifty years."

"And we know what lives in a chicken house."

"Do we?"

"Um-hmm." He leaned toward me and whispered, "Chickens!"

I laughed in his face. "This is good, Pete. After all these years, you've figured out that chickens live in a slurpen house. You know what else? Horses live in the horse pasture."

"Don't try to change the subject, Hankie. You came up here for a special reason, didn't you?"

"I don't know what you're talking about."

"Chickens, Hankie. Were you thinking about chickens? Be honest."

I turned away from him. "Why would you ask such a ridiculous question?"

"Well, Hankie, you may not know this, but your every thought shows up on your face. It's like reading a neon sign."

"What are you saying, cat?"

He batted his eyes. "I'm saying, Hankie, that you came up here for a chicken dinner and it's written all over your face. Tell me I'm wrong."

I marched a few steps away. All at once I had a powerful desire to, uh, hide my thoughts. "You're not only wrong, you're crazy. Why would I be thinking about a chicken dinner?"

"Well, let me think. Because you're hungry. Because Sally May isn't watching. Because you're a dog and therefore a slave to your appetites. Shall I go on, Hankie?"

"No, that's plenty." I marched back to him. "It's all rubbish, Pete, rubbish and lies, just the sort of junk that comes from the mouth of cat who has too much time on his hands."

"Oh really? Watch this." He looked me in the eyes and whispered, "Chicken dinner!" Slurp. For some reason, my, uh, tongue shot out and licked my lips. "Chicken dinner!" It happened again. Slurp. "What do you say now, Hankie?"

"I say it proves almost nothing at all, is what I say."

"Oh really? Try it on me."

I glared down at the scheming little fraud. "Okay, buddy, you asked for this. Chicken dinner!"

Oops. Somehow it . . . uh . . . backfired, you might say. Pete yawned and I was the one who licked his chops. Slurp. It happened before I knew it, I mean, the old tongue just popped out and did its work.

This was embarrassing. I mean, a guy never wants to admit that a cat might be right about anything, and when the cat really *is* right, it's even worse.

"What do you say now, Hankie?"

My mind was tumbling. At last I came up with the perfect response. "Okay, Pete, up the tree."

"Now, Hankie . . ."

"Up the tree, you little pestilence!"

He didn't move, so I barked in his face, another of my Train Horns applications. Heh heh. He arched his back and hissed and . . . okay, maybe he landed a lucky punch to the end of my nose . . . several lucky punches. They hurt like crazy but I didn't care. The important thing is that I chased him twenty yards to the west and ran him up a chinaberry tree.

"There! And let that be a lesson to you."

He smirked down at me. "What's the lesson, Hankie?"

"The lesson is that when you try to mess with the mind of a dog, you pay a terrible price."

"But Hankie, it's so much fun! And so easy."

"Oh yeah? Well, try it again sometime and we'll just see what happens."

He batted his eyes. *Chicken dinner.*

Slurp.

Never mind the rest. I had parked the local cat in a tree and had served the cause of justice. Holding my head at a proud angle, I marched away from the scene, knowing in my deepest heart that I had won another huge moral victory over the cat.

I made my way down the hill toward the . . . boy, a guy forgets how much damage a cat can do with those claws. Ouch. I made my way down the hill, strolled into the lobby of the Security Division's Vast Office Complex, and rode the elevator up to the twelfth floor.

There, I found my assistant standing with his nose in the corner. When I entered the office, he pulled away from the corner and gave me his usual silly grin. "Oh goodie, my time's up."

"Your time's not up. Get back in the corner."

"Oh drat."

I fluffed up my gunnysack bed, did three turns around it, and collapsed. "Ah yes, this is the good life: peace, quiet, and a loving gunnysack! Drover, hold my calls and good night." I stretched out on my bed and prepared to release my grip on the world.

"What happened to your nose?"

I cracked open one eye. "I beg your pardon?"

"What happened to your nose?"

"Drover, what makes you think something happened to my nose?"

"Well, it looks all beat up."

I lifted my head and beamed him a glare. "If you must know, I wrecked a cat and in the process, I sustained a few minor cuts and bruises."

"They look pretty major to me."

"They're minor, a small price to pay for humbling the cat. Good night." Again, I closed my eyes and began floating out onto a sea of . . .

"I'm getting a crick in my neck."

"I don't care."

"Can I take my nose out of the corner?"

"No."

"I hate this!"

"Remember that next time you're templed to mouse off to a spearior ossifer . . . snork murk."

"Are you asleep?"

"Huh?"

"What's that sound? Hank?"

With great effort, I raised my head and cranked open the outer doors of my eyes. I blinked several times and glanced around. "Where are we?"

"Oh, under the gas tanks, our same old bedroom. I guess you fell asleep."

"Yes, of course." Suddenly my left ear shot up. "Drover, I don't want to alarm you, but I'm picking up an odd sound."

"Yeah, that's what I said."

"No, two odd sounds: the hum of a distant motor and also a certain crackling sound."

I jacked myself up to a standing position and homed in on the mysterious sounds. They seemed to be coming from the direction of the corrals.

Fire in
the Hole!

"Drover, someone is operating a welder, and I have a vague memory that we've been through this before."

"I'll be derned. I wonder who it could be."

"Hang on and I'll run diagnostics." I narrowed my eyes into the setting for Long Range Viewing. "I think it's Slim. He's welding." A scowl settled over my brow and I began pacing, as I often do when I'm facing complex problems. "Drover, were we observing Slim earlier in the day? If so, why did we leave and what are we doing here?"

"I can't think when my neck hurts."

"All right, you're relieved."

"Boy, that's a relief!"

He removed his nose from the corner, while I paced back and forth in front of him. Something about this deal didn't add up.

"Drover, this troubles me. In this dry weather, Slim shouldn't be welding. It's a fragrant violation of all our fire codes."

"Flagrant."

"What?"

"You said fragrant, but you meant flagrant."

"Don't bore me with details. If Slim is welding, we should be down there, watching for fires and enforcing the codes. Why are we just sitting here in the office?"

He squinted one eye and rolled the other one up toward the sky. "You know, I don't remember. Sometimes I forget things."

I stopped pacing and cut my eyes from side to side. "Are you sure we weren't down there earlier in the day?"

"Boy, everything's a blur."

"You need to work on your memory."

"I know but I keep forgetting to do it."

"Well"—I took a deep breath and filled my air tanks—"we'd better get back on the job. Stand by for launch!"

"Oh goodie, I'm starved."

"Drover, I said *launch,* not lunch."

"Oh drat. You mean . . ."

"Yes. It's time to launch all dogs, and please stop talking about food."

"You're not hungry?"

"No." At that very moment a picture of chicken-on-a-plate flashed across the mentality of my mind. Slurp. "Yes, I'm hungry, but we have work to do. Come on, soldier, let's move out. Head up, tail up . . . march!"

Boy, you should have seen us. We formed a column and marched to the beet of a distant turnip, through the saddle lot, the wire lot, and the sorting alley. Heads high and proud, we marched past Slim, who was working beside the cow chute.

He raised his welding hood and watched us with a puzzled smile. "What's this? Dogs on parade?"

Right, Dogs on Parade. We had come to show solidarity with dogs all over the world, dogs who were fed up with careless fire-bug cowboys, dogs who had joined together to protest the injustice of everything unjust.

As I marched past him, I turned my head and gave him a glare that said, "Thought you could sneak down here and run the welder in violation of Title Five of the Fire Code, huh? Bad news, fella. We're here to investigate."

Pretty impressive, huh? You bet. I got him told and the guy was left speechless. I mean, what could he say in the face of such . . .

Huh?

He lowered the welding hood, covering his face. His arms rose slowly in the air and his hands . . . yipes, his fingers spread into gnarled clawlike claws and . . .

I heard Drover squeak behind me. "Hank, I remember now. We were down here a while ago and he turned into a robot monster!"

"Roger that, but maybe it's just a trick. He's done this before, you know. We will now make an orderly retreat to the west fence and try to remain calm."

We suspended the parade and withdrew our troops about fifty feet to the west, where we huddled against the corral fence and . . . well, continued to monitor the situation. I was pretty sure this was Slim playing pranks again, but when a guy's in charge of the safety of his troops, he can't afford to take chances.

I was thinking mainly of Drover. You know how he is.

Pressing our bodies against the fence, we waited and watched. The creature raised the hood and . . . see, I told you. The face belonged to Slim

Chance, and he was grinning like . . . I don't know what. Like a possum. Like a monkey.

He said, "Hi, puppies. Did I fool you again? Tell the truth."

I beamed him a scorching glare that said, "You did not fool us, we know all about your silly pranks, and we'd appreciate it if you would stop goofing off!"

At last he did. He had to. After you've done the same trick five times in a row, the audience loses interest. I was embarrassed for him. I mean, what can you say about a grown man who wastes half the afternoon trying to terrorize his dogs? It was pathetic.

Slim lowered his hood and started welding again, only this time I was there to supervise his every move. I studied the red and yellow sparks that were landing around his feet, while the drone of the welding motor echoed through my ear canals.

Let me tell you something about welding. For a while it's kind of interesting—you know, the smoke cloud, the flash of light, the shower of sparks and so forth—but after about five minutes, time begins to drag. A lot of dogs would close their eyes and star fall sleep and snicklefritz hog report on Tuesday . . .

Huh? Sorry, my wand mandered . . . my mind wandered there for a second and I almose driffled off to puddle murfing snork burf snizzle piffle sponk . . . zzzzzzzzz.

Huh? Okay, I was having a little tribble coping my eyes eepen . . . a little trouble keeping my eyes open, let us say. I mean, all at once my eyelids seemed to have lead weights attached . . . zzzzt . . . lead eyes attached to my doorknobs and my head kept dripping down on my checkerboard . . . my head kept dropping down on my . . . zzzzzzzzz.

Huh? Where was I? Okay, welding. You want the straight story on welding? It's nothing a dog would ever do because any dog with an active mind would die of boredom in ten minutes. Duty demanded that we maintain a presence with Slim while he was working, but I muss admip that . . . zzzzzzzzzzzz.

"Hank, you'd better wake up!"

Had I heard a voice? Yes. Had I wanted to hear a voice? No. Therefore, the voice I had heard was not a voice at all. It had actually been some kind of . . . carrot cracker pumping happy squash bugs . . .

"Hank, wake up! There's something you need to see."

I cranked open one eyelid. It weighed five thousand pounds. I held it open long enough to see . . . who was that? I summoned a burst of energy and cranked open the other eye, revealing the same guy I'd seen with the first eye.

Okay, it was Drover. I blinked several times and glanced around. "Drivver, somebody was calling my name."

"Yeah, it was me."

"Okay, that checks out because, well, there you are."

"Yeah, but my name's Drover. You called me Drivver."

"I did not call you Drivver. My splurch was sleed . . . my speech was slurred, that's all, and why are you bothering me in the middle of my nap?"

"Well, there's a fire, right over there."

I hauled myself up to a standing position and shook the vapors out of my head.

HUH? "Drover, I don't want to alarm you, but those dry weeds around the cow chute seem to be burning."

"Yeah, I know."

"Ignited by sparks from Slim's welder."

"Yeah, that's what I was trying to tell you."

I whirled around and gave him a ferocious glare. "Drover, the weeds at Slim's feet are on fire and he doesn't know it! Why didn't you wake me up and tell me?"

"Well, I think I just did."

I shook more vapors out of my head. "Well, someone should warn Slim, don't you think?"

"Yeah, that's what I thought."

"Then do it! What are you waiting for?"

"Well . . ." He took a couple of limping steps. "To tell you the truth, this old leg's been giving me fits again."

"Oh brother! Never mind, you little faker, I'll handle it myself." I pushed him out of the way and hurried over to the cow chute. I waited a moment, figuring that Slim would notice me. He didn't and I could understand why. I mean, the welder was roaring so loud he couldn't hear anything, and he was working inside that hood and couldn't see much either.

I didn't want to interrupt his work, but the fire at his feet was growing larger by the moment and, well, someone needed to take some action. I took a deep breath of air and barked. No response. I moved closer and barked again, louder this time.

"May I have your attention please! We interrupt this program to bring you a special news

bulletin. Fire Patrol has located a small fire in the vicinity of your boots. At the present time it's not causing any great damage, but that could change at any moment. Hello? Do you read me?"

I waited. The welder roared, sparks flew, and Slim was off in another world. Okay, I would have to crank up the barking. I inched closer, filled my lungs with a huge gulp of air, and cut loose with a burst of Rude and Intrusive Barking.

Oof!

You won't believe this. The guy was standing in a circle of fire, but when I tried to give him a warning, he reached out his big ugly steel-toed boot and kicked me! Okay, that did it. I marched away and joined Drover at the corral fence.

He gave me a worried look. "Gosh, I wonder if his pants legs could catch on fire."

"I don't know and I don't care."

"His cuffs are kind of ragged. See all those strings?"

"I see the strings, Drover, and if I were wearing those coveralls, I would be worried, but I'm not. When these people ignore their dogs, they have to take the consequences."

We watched and, sure enough, one of the strings on Slim's ragged cuff caught fire. Then another. In seconds, the whole cuff burst into flames. Drover turned to me with a look of alarm.

"Hank?"

"Drover, I did my best and nothing worked. It's hopeless."

"There's one thing left."

I stared at him. "What's left?"

"Bite 'im!"

CHAPTER FIVE

I Rescue Slim from a Burning Pants Leg

Drover's words hung in the air like words hanging in the air.

"Bite him? Are you crazy?"

We watched as the flames on his cuffs grew larger. "Hank, you'd better do something, and quick!"

I heaved a sigh and rose to my feet. "Okay, I'm going in—not because he deserves it but because . . . I don't know why. Because this is what dogs do. You come in the second wave."

"And do what?"

"I don't know, spit on the flames or something. Lend a hand, break a leg."

"I already did." He limped around in circles and fell over. "There it went! Oh, my leg!"

I stepped over his twitching body and prepared for action. This would be one of the most dangerous missions of my entire career and I knew there was a good chance that I would run into trouble. To get Slim's attention, I would have to bite him hard enough to get his attention, and he wouldn't like that. Oh well, it had to be done.

I entered all the targeting information and locked it into the computer. The target was acquired. We were ready to launch. I rolled the muscles in my enormous shoulders and pointed my nose directly at the target. While Drover squeaked and quivered, I launched the weapon.

"Charge, bonzai!"

Boy, old Slim was sure surprised! I mean, there he was, a happy bachelor cowboy doing his fix-up job on the cow chute, all alone in his little world under the welding hood, and totally unaware that his pants were on fire, when all at once a four-legged cruise missile came out of nowhere and took a bite out of his hip pocket.

SNAP!

I knew right away that I had gotten his attention. "Eeeeee-YOW!" He jumped about five feet straight up, banged his head on a chute lever, and then everything became a blur of motion. Off came the welding hood, off came the leather

gloves. Welding rods, slag hammer, marking chalk, tape measure, and electric cords went flying in all directions.

He grabbed his hiney with both hands and with a very astonished expression on his face, he screamed, "IDIOT! YOU BIT ME!"

Right. And your pants are on fire.

His face had become a mask of rage. He lunged toward me, and this time he wasn't playing games. I think he had plans for twisting my head off, but then he began to feel the heat from his flaming pants.

He stopped dead in his tracks and stared at the fire coming up his leg. His mouth dropped open and I heard him say, "Good honk, I'm on fire!" Then he started dancing a polka and slapping at the flames. "Hyah, hyah!"

Well, glory be, he'd finally figured it out. These guys take a lot of patience, but once in a while we're rewarded with a successful mission.

He moved with a kind of speed we'd never seen before. After he'd stomped out the fire in the weeds, down came the zipper on his coveralls. He wiggled his shoulders and flopped his arms and waggled the top half of his body around, dropped to the ground and kicked his legs until the coveralls finally came flying off.

They landed in a heap nearby and roared up into a blaze big enough to roast a couple of goats and a bunch of marshmallows. Slim just sat there and watched, stunned and amazed, while his welding uniform went up in smoke.

After a bit he chuckled and turned his eyes on me. "Pooch, it ain't polite to bite your friends, but I'm kind of glad you did this time. I guess I owe you one. Thanks."

Yes, he certainly "owed me one" and I waited for the awards ceremony to begin. What would it be? A big juicy steak? A package of frozen hamburger from the deep freeze? Or maybe a whole gallon of ice cream, all to myself? Any of those items would have been fine with me or, what the heck, all of them would have been even better.

I mean, let's look at the facts. My rescue had been so rapid and well-timed, the fire hadn't even burned his jeans, much less his leg, so, yes, this seemed a perfect time for him to give me a huge reward.

He reached two fingers into his shirt pocket and dug around. He frowned. "Well, I thought I still had a piece of beef jerky but I guess I ate it for lunch. Will you take an IOU?"

What? An IOU? No! I wanted my steak! Our

dog bowl had been empty for two weeks! Okay, twelve hours, but it had been empty.

He grinned. "Thanks, pooch, I knew you'd understand. An IOU from an honest man is almost as good as a sack of gold."

Oh sure, and an IOU from a crook was almost as good as a sack of gold without the gold.

He yawned. "Well, it's quittin' time anyway. You want to stay down at my place tonight?"

No, I certainly did not. I had better things to do and better friends to do it with. I turned my back on him and went into a Deep Sulk.

"Hey, I'll give you a bite of my mackerel and ketchup sandwich."

No. I was hungry but not desperate.

He shrugged. "No? Well, I'll think of you when I'm eating my supper. Nighty night."

And with that, he slouched off to his pickup and drove away, leaving me in the ruins of a shattered steak dream.

You know, if dogs wrote the history books, there would be a lot of embarrassed humans. We would tell all about their childish pranks and bonehead mistakes, about how they goof off and play robot on company time and catch their clothes on fire.

Oh well. Darkness was approaching, and Drover and I made our way back to our office/bedroom underneath the gas tanks. It had turned into a pretty strenuous afternoon, with all the monster reports, fire alarms, and shattered dreams, and I was ready for some shut-eye. As I was scratching up my gunnysack bed, I noticed Drover staring at me.

"What?"

"Oh nothing. I was just thinking."

"That's scary. About what?"

"You sure saved old Slim. What a hero!"

"Right, what a hero, and what did it get me? A pat on the head. At the very least, he should have given me a steak dinner."

"Yeah, but he's too cheap."

My head shot up and so did my ears. I gazed out into the darkness. "Did you hear that?"

"I didn't hear anything."

"Well, I did. It was that same bird we heard earlier."

He giggled. "Oh, you mean 'cheap'?"

Slurp.

"Yes. You heard it, too?" I leaped to my feet. "Drover, unless I'm badly mistaken, there's a young, tender chicken out there in the darkness!"

"No, it was just me. I said—"

"I can't stand this any longer. Every time I try to relax, I hear chickens! They're everywhere and it's driving me crazy." I turned my fevered gaze upon my assistant. "I have to settle this thing, once and for all."

"Yeah, but—"

"Don't wait up for me, son. This could turn into a late night."

"Yeah, but—"

I didn't stick around to hear the rest of his "yeah, but." I went plunging into the darkness of night, in search of . . .

I know what you're thinking: I had become possessed with the thought of eating a chicken. Go ahead and admit it. You think I had turned into some kind of chicken-killing fiend, right?

Okay, maybe you've got a point, but let's look at it from another angle. We're not talking about a whole bunch of chickens, just one, and who would miss one little chicken? Nobody. Chickens come and go, right? They have accidents and, well, sometimes they just vanish without a trace. It happens all the time.

And don't forget that the people who operate the ranch had forgotten to refill our dog bowl. Was that my fault? What's a dog to do? I mean, we sit around all day, listening to the wildcats growling in our stomachs and watching as two-legged dinners walk around in front of us, and what are we supposed to think about? The weather? Volcanic activity in Washington State? Fungus and algae?

Look, dogs aren't saints. When we're hungry, we think about FOOD, and when we see plump juicy chickens . . . slurp . . . walking around all day, we begin thinking the unthinkable.

And don't forget that I hadn't been paid for my heroic rescue of Slim. I deserved a special treat, and by George . . .

Yes, I'll admit that inviting one of Sally May's chickens to supper involved . . . uh, certain risks, shall we say. But I had a plan and it didn't involve Sally May's approval . . . or knowledge.

Heh heh. *Hide the feathers and they'll never know.* Heh heh. Yes sir, I was a dog with a plan. I can't reveal it at this time (it's highly classified), but you'll see.

Oh, one last thing. You're probably disappointed that I was taking this swerve into antisocial behavior. I'm sorry to disappoint you, but I never pretended to be a perfect dog. Through the years, I've tried to be a good dog, but even good dogs yield to temptation every once in a while, and there's no temptation like a plump, juicy . . .

Slurp.

That's all I'm going to say about it. If this next part gets unbearable, just skip a couple of chapters and we'll see you on the other side.

CHAPTER SIX

A Plunge into Darkest Darkness

Okay, where were we? Oh yes, I had stormed out of the office and had entered the world outside where darkness and temptation lurked behind every bush and tree. I felt the darkness, both inside and out, and believe it or not, all at once I began hearing a creepy song in the back of my mind. No kidding. Here, listen to this.

Chickens

Chickens . . . all I see are chickens.
It really is the dickens
When the mind plays clever tricks,
Projecting colored pictures
Of a bird upon a plate.
Such a cruel fate!

Dinners . . . all I see are dinners.
Just exactly what a sinner
Doesn't need. It's so frustrating
To see roasted birds parading
Down the Broadway of my mind.
Destiny's unkind!

On the other hand, it's really kind of neat
to have these visions.
It provides a little break between
decisions.
Don't forget, a guy needs rest,
A break from all the stress
Of working day and night to earn his pay.

Sleeping . . . Sally May is sleeping.
And while she sleeps I'm creeping
Like a panther through a park,
At ease in total darkness.
A phantom in the night,
But still aware it isn't right.

Lurking . . . images are lurking.
I hear the sounds of slurping
In the river of my mouth.
My life is going south,

For if I should get caught,
I'd have to eat these chicken thoughts.

On the other hand, there's a kind of
    peace of mind that I am needing.
It's the calm that soothes the conscience
    after eating.
Good digestion forms a link
To what we do and think,
'Cause nourishment is part of mental
    health.

Chickens . . .

Pretty spooky song, huh? I thought so, but it
sort of expressed the situation in which I found
myself.

I made my way toward . . . do I dare reveal my
destination? I guess it wouldn't hurt, and you've
probably already guessed it anyway.

The chicken house. If a guy wishes to mug a
chicken after sundown, that's where he goes, because that's where chickens roost at night.

It was very dark out there and I had switched
my instruments over to Smelloradar, but then
I noticed a flash of light off to the northwest. It

appeared to be lightning inside a line of thunder-clouds. This promised to be either good news or bad news: good news if it brought rain, bad news if we got lightning and no rain.

See, dry lightning is a major cause of prairie fires, and don't forget that our country was dry, very dry. I made a mental note to keep an eye on those clouds, once I had taken care of my, uh, business.

Slurp.

I crept through the darkness, up the hill to the flat area where the chicken house stood about twenty yards southwest of the machine shed. I paused to reconoodle the situation, cocked my left ear, and listened. Not a sound, except . . . okay, relax. It was just a distant thumber of rundle.

Rumble of thunder, let us say, but nothing to worry about. I paused long enough to grab a quick gulp of air, knowing that I would need plenty of air to . . . well, to do what I was fixing to do, and we needn't dwell on that.

I turned my nose toward the dark outline of the chicken house and began my stealthy march toward . . .

"Mmmmm. Hello, Hankie."

I froze in my tracks. The voice had come from

somewhere above my present location. I lifted my eyes to the first branch of a chinaberry tree and saw . . . would you like to guess? Pete.

The air hissed out of my lungs. "You again? Don't you have anything better to do than lurk in trees?"

"Not really, Hankie. See, I knew you'd be back and I decided to wait right here. Just as I suspected, you came back."

"Okay, Pete, you get an A for being a snoop. You're the champ, so watch all you want and enjoy the show."

"Actually, Hankie, I've been thinking about your situation."

I studied his silhouette in the tree. He was sharpening his claws on a limb. "I didn't know I had a 'situation.'"

"Of course you do. It's just dawned on me that you're out of dog food, you poor thing. Why didn't you tell me?"

"I didn't consider it any of your business, kitty, and I still don't. Now, if you'll excuse me . . ."

"But Hankie, don't you see? This changes everything." He stopped clawing the limb and sat with his tail curled around his haunches. "It explains why you're going to the chicken house. I had no idea!"

I moved to the base of the tree and studied him for a moment. I noticed that he wasn't smirking, which came as a shock. I couldn't remember the last time I'd seen Pete without an insolent smirk wrapped around his mouth.

"What's your point, kitty, or do you have a point?"

"Actually, Hankie, I do." He leaned out on the limb and said, "I can help!"

HUH?

His words went through me like a jolt of electricity. At first I was stunned, then I heard myself laughing. "Oh, that's rich, Pete! Ha ha. After years of being a pestilence, you've decided to *help*? Ha ha! Sorry, pal, I don't believe it."

He wasn't laughing. "I know, Hankie, I never thought I'd be so moved by . . ." He turned his eyes toward heaven. "Well, by the spectacle of a loyal dog going hungry for a whole day. It's . . . it's so very sad."

I glanced over both shoulders, just to make sure that Drover wasn't listening to this. I mean, carrying on friendly conversations with cats was strictly against regulations. "Pete, you'll have to forgive me for not believing this. See, you're a cat and cats never think of anyone but themselves."

He heaved a sigh. "I know, Hankie, we are

inclined that way. All I can say is"—holy smokes, he seemed to be fighting back tears!—"your situation has touched my heart."

Gee, what does a guy say to that? I had to sit down. "Pete, don't cry. I mean, I haven't been starving or anything, but now you understand the strain I've been under . . . with the chickens and everything."

"I do, Hankie, I do! I don't know how you've been able to hold yourself back."

"Well, it's been tough, Pete. I won't deny it. And I want the record to show that eating a chicken wasn't my first choice of things to do."

"I understand, I do. It's so sad that your human friends have pushed you into this. But Hankie, I want you to know that *you deserve a chicken!*"

Wow. I was speechless. I mean, the scheming little reptile . . . Pete, I should say, had put it even better than I could have: I deserved a chicken! It took me several seconds to recover from the shock.

"Pete, I must ask you a question. Are you being sincere about this? I mean, I'd really be mad if this turned out to be another of your tricks."

Get this. He sat up straight and placed a paw over his heart. "On my Honor as a Cat, Hankie, I

swear by everything sacred and holy . . . that you'd be really mad if this turned out to be a trick."

Wow again. The cat had sworn a sacred oath and I couldn't believe I'd heard it. This had never happened on our ranch before, never.

After a moment of stunned silence, I managed to say, "Well, that settles it. I guess we'll be working together on this job, pardner. You don't mind if I call you 'pardner,' do you?"

He came slithering down the tree. "Oh no! In fact, I think it has a nice ring to it."

He came over to me and started rubbing on my legs. As you know, I don't care for that, but . . . what the heck, we had just entered a new chapter in our relationship and if my pardner wanted to rub on my legs, that was okay.

"What did you have in mind, Pete?"

He stopped rubbing and glanced over both shoulders. Then he leaned toward me and whispered behind his paw. "You'll need me to unlock the chicken house door."

"I will?"

"Oh yes. For the past two weeks, Sally May has been bolting the chicken house door. Didn't you know that?"

Huh? I turned away, so that he couldn't see the

shock on my face. "I didn't say that. Of course I knew it. What's your point?"

"Yes. She's seen some footprints around there, and she's afraid that someone is going to get in. Anyway, the point is"—he raised a paw and wiggled his toes—"I know how to open the bolt."

"So you're saying . . ."

He fluttered his eyelids and grinned. "I'll throw the bolt and hold the door open while you do your business. When you're outside again, I'll bolt it shut . . . and nobody will ever suspect a thing!"

I couldn't help being impressed. "Well, you think of everything, Pete. Nobody schemes better than a cat."

"You can bet on that."

"I beg your pardon?"

"I said, thank you, Hankie. Your trust really astounds me."

I patted him on the back. "Well, that's what this life is all about, Pete, trusting each other and working together. Let's get this over with. To be honest, I'm a little nervous."

"You should be."

"Right. I mean, this goes against all my training and instincts. I hope you understand that."

"Oh, I do, I do."

Pretty amazing, huh? You bet. Who would have thought that Pete and I would end up working on the same team . . . or that it would be *his* idea? He was just a dumb little ranch cat, but I guess he'd finally figured out that playing on a winning team is always a winner.

We slipped through the darkness and made not a sound, and I had to give Pete some credit there. The guy was good at the stealthy stuff, and I was impressed that he didn't seem the least bit nervous. In fact, the old Kitty Smirk had returned to his mouth, only now he was putting it to good use—smirking for Our Team.

We crept up to the little door on the north side of the chicken house. As you may recall, there were two entrances, a big door for people and a smaller one near the ground that the chickens used. The smaller entrance had a hinged door that opened one way, to the outside. In the mornings, Sally May wired it open so that the chickens could go outside and spend the day chasing bugs. In the evenings, she shut them up again, to protect them from . . . uh, bad guys.

That little door would be my Entry Point into the Target Area. Our most recent satellite pictures had revealed that Sally May had started bolting the door, see, and that's why I had hired an assistant to help with the job. Heh heh. Was that clever or what?

We stopped beside the chicken entrance and I studied the door. Sure enough, there was a new brass device with a sliding bolt, just as our satellite imagery had predicted. Everything checked out and we were ready. I took one last look around. The sky was dark and quiet except for an occasional flash of lightning and thumder of rundle.

"Okay, pardner, I guess we're ready. You lift the door and hold it open. I'll snatch a bird and run. Make sure nothing goes wrong. It wouldn't be funny if I got trapped in there." I heard something that sounded like muffled laughter.

"You're right, Hankie. That wouldn't be . . . pfffft . . . funny at all. Hee hee."

"Are you laughing?"

"It's a backward laugh, Hankie. It means that this is not . . . tee hee . . . funny at all."

"Oh. Good. You know, Pete, if this works out, I may find a little job for you in the Security Division. We could start you out working a couple of days a week, sweeping floors and hauling trash. How does that sound?"

For some reason, he couldn't speak. Maybe the thought of working with the Security Division had just overwhelmed him, and I could understand that. I mean, how many cats get such a great opportunity?

"Okay, Pete, we've got a Go for the mission. Stay alert and I'll see you on the other side."

"Pffft . . . hee ha . . . pffffft!"

You know, cats make odd sounds sometimes. They're strange, even the good ones.

CHAPTER SEVEN

Conned by
a Cat

Pete loosened up his claws, I mean, he looked like a professional safecracker or something. This cat was good. He slid the bolt and lifted the door. I crawled through the opening.

It was pretty small, you know, just right for a chicken but small for a dog with enormous shoulders. Once inside, I rose to my feet and listened. Not a sound. Okay, a few sounds: the regular breathing patterns of twenty-eight chickens and an occasional snore.

Did you know that chickens snore in their sleep? I can't say that I knew it, and for good reason. I had spent very little time in the company of sleeping chickens.

I reached for the microphone of my mind and

made one last check-in. "Lunar Module to base, how does everything look out there, over?"

"Just swell, Hankie, except for one small problem."

"Oh?"

"Uh-huh. It's the door, Hankie."

"What about the door?"

"Well, I'm having a little trouble holding it open."

That sent a jolt down my spine. "What? Hold it open! Do you copy?"

"But Hankie, it's heavy and I'm getting bored."

I felt the blood rushing to my face, causing my eyes to bulge outward. *"Moron, I don't care if you're getting . . ."* The words died in my throat. I cut my eyes from side to side as new and terrible thoughts began marching across the parade ground of my mind. "Hey Pete, we need to talk."

"No we don't, Hankie."

"Yes, we do. This afternoon, we had a little argument, remember? We exchanged a few, well, harsh words, and I, uh, ran you up a tree. Listen, pal, I've been thinking about that."

"Uh-huh. Me too, Hankie, all afternoon."

"Right, and it's becoming clear that I might have . . . well, come across a little too strong. Abrasive."

"Rude and unfriendly?"

"Exactly, Pete, and . . . well, it's bothering me. I mean, we dogs sometimes do and say things that we later regret. Pete, I'm experiencing some . . . some remorse for my rude behavior. No kidding."

"Heavy remorse?"

"Oh yes, definitely. It's really, uh, pressing down on my spirit."

There was a moment of eerie silence. "Does that mean you're sorry?"

I flinched on that word. I mean, it hurt like a cactus spine in the foot. "That's getting close, Pete, but could we choose a different word? To be honest, I have a problem saying 'I'm sorry.'"

"Poor doggie."

"Right. See, I've always found it hard to say it out loud."

"Mmmm. To anyone, Hankie, or just to cats?"

I paused to think about my response. I knew this would be crucial. "To everyone, Pete, but especially to cats. I guess it's kind of irrational, but . . . ha ha . . . it's the truth. It has something to do with being a dog, I guess."

"I guess it does. Well, Hankie, let me suggest another word."

I breathed a sigh of relief. "Pete, I knew we could work this out."

"Let me suggest . . . *dumb.*"

"Huh? Dumb? Did I hear you right?"

"Dumb. You had your chance and you blew it."

The door slammed shut. The bolt slid into place. I rushed to the door and pushed. It didn't move. *Pete had . . .*

My mouth was suddenly very dry. Behind me in the darkness, several chickens clucked. I spoke to the closed door.

"Hey Pete, let's back up and start all over again. Okay, I've thought it over and I'm ready to say, 'I'm sorry.' Pete, are you listening? Hello?" No response. I leaped to the door and began banging on it with my paws. "Traitor! Open this door and let me out of here!"

I was trapped.

I slumped to the floor and blinked my eyes, trying to absorb the calamity that had just fallen upon me. I had trusted the treacherous, scheming little snake, and now he had . . .

The clucking of the chickens grew louder, and in the gloomy half-light, I could see them standing up on their nests, staring at me with big chicken eyes. I could tell that they wondered what . . . well, what a dog was doing inside their chicken house . . . after dark.

My mind was racing. I had to do something, and fast!

I struggled to my feet, gave the chickens a smile of greatest sincerity, and spoke in a soothing voice.

"Hi there. My name's Joey and I'm going to be your tour guide. You may not believe this, but we're riding in a bus. See, you all signed up for our annual Fall Foliage Tour and, well, I'm here to see that you have a wonderful time. Ha ha."

Were they buying my story? It was hard to say. Chickens look stupid, no matter what they're doing, and these birds fit the pattern. But at least they weren't squawking and flapping their wings.

I mushed on. Walking slowly down the aisle, I pointed to the north wall. "Out this window, we see several groves of chinaberry trees, sometimes called the western soapberry. They are native to our area and they're always the first to turn golden yellow in the fall. Aren't they lovely?"

The chickens looked toward the blank wall, then back to me. I had no idea where this was going, but I had to keep talking until I could come up with a better plan.

I pointed to the south wall. "And out this window, we see our most graceful tree, the

cottonwood. Fall in the Texas Panhandle wouldn't be the same without our cottonwoods. When their leaves begin to turn, when we hear the honking of geese and cranes overhead, we know that winter isn't far behind."

Just then a clap of thunder grumbled outside. Lousy luck! The chickens exchanged looks of alarm and began muttering. I had to act fast. "Uh . . . the show's up here, folks, eyes this way, please! Thank you. I'm sure you have many questions, and I'd be glad to answer them."

A scowling rooster at the rear raised his wing. It was J.T. Cluck, and he said, "You're name ain't Joey, pooch, and this ain't a bus."

I tried to swallow the poisonous taste in my mouth. The tension was rising. They were all staring at me, waiting to hear what I would say.

"Great point, J.T., very perceptive. Okay, we're not actually on a foliage tour and you're right, this isn't your average tour bus. Ha ha. It's not a bus at all and you've probably figured out that I'm your Head of Ranch Security."

Someone in the audience yelled, "We knew this wasn't a bus. You didn't fool us!"

I tried to calm them with a gentle laugh. "Ha ha. Listen, would you believe that I'm actually here on a secret mission?"

I held my breath and waited for their response. It came in a loud chorus. "NO!"

"All right, let's cut to the bottom line. I blundered in here by mistake and a scheming little cat locked the door. I would like nothing better than to get out of here and leave you in peace. Is there another exit?"

The chickens muttered and clucked among themselves, while I listened to the pounding of my heart. At last, their eyes swung back to me, and J.T. said, "Pooch, we've just figured it out. *We've got a dog in our chicken house!*"

My spirits dropped like a chunk of cement. "Right, and what we need to do is remain calm."

What a joke. Remain calm? Suddenly the room erupted in wild shrieks and hysterical clucking, as chickens flapped their wings, flew into walls, fainted, and screeched like . . . I don't know what. Like a room full of hysterical, brainless chickens who had gone berserk over nothing. Idiot birds.

Oh brother. I was cooked. I staggered through the blizzard of floating feathers and screaming chickens and sat down beside the door. I knew that within minutes, the big door would open and I would find myself looking into the flaming eyes of . . . someone, Loper or Sally May.

Gulp.

With nothing better to do, I began rehearsing my story. "Sally May, I know this looks bad, a dog in the, uh, chicken house after lights-out. In fact, it looks *very* bad and no one is more aware of it than me. Frankly, I can't remember ever being in a more awkward situation in my whole life. All I can tell you is . . . *I have no idea how I got here.* Honest. No kidding. You'll just have to trust me on that."

Would it sell? I didn't have long to wait. Minutes later, the hinges on the big door squeaked, sending stabs of terror down my backbone. The door swung open and I turned my gaze toward . . .

Holy smokes, you won't believe this. It wasn't Sally May, the most dreaded ranch wife in Ochiltree County, and it wasn't even her husband. It was my very best pal in the whole world . . . Little Alfred! He hadn't gone to bed yet!

"Hankie, what are you doing in here?"

I flew into his arms with a rush of gratitude. Oh, happy day! Oh, sweet salvation! Alfred would never believe all the terrible lies and rumors about me. He would understand that I had always wanted to be a good dog and that . . . well, strange things happen in this world.

I raised up on my back legs and began licking every square inch of his face, neck, and ears. The boy had earned it and I held nothing back. But then my heart was frozen by a man's voice in the distance.

"Alfred? Son, what is it?"

Yipes, it was Loper, coming out the yard gate! I gave the boy an urgent look that said, "Alfred, I think I can explain everything . . . later. Right now, I'd better get out of here. Thanks, pal!"

I went straight into Turbo Five and vanished into the night . . . into the machine shed, actually. There, I watched as Loper's flashlight moved up the hill and across the gravel drive.

"Alfred? What got the chickens stirred up?"

The boy walked toward his dad. "Well . . . there was something in the chicken house."

"An animal?"

"Uh-huh."

I held my breath. I knew the lad didn't want to rat on me, but his dad pushed for more details. "A skunk? A coon?"

The boy clasped his hands behind his back and looked up at the moon. "Well . . . it was awful dark, Dad. Maybe it was a . . . a tiger."

A tiger, yes! Great answer. We could do a lot with that. A wild tiger had broken out of its cage . . . in a traveling carnival . . . yes, a carnival that had stopped for a few days in Twitchell. In the middle of the night, this terrible beast had ripped the bars out of its cage and . . .

Uh-oh. Loper was walking toward the chicken house, shining his light on the ground. Oops. Remember what we said about the dry weather? Dry weather makes dust and dust makes tracks. Gulp.

Loper studied the ground for a long time, then . . . "Son, did you find a dog in the chicken house?"

The boy lowered his eyes and nodded. "Yes sir."

"Which dog? Never mind, I already know." He opened the chicken house door and shined his light inside. "Well, I don't see any blood. He must have botched the job."

"Dad, maybe he got lonesome."

"Ha ha. I'll bet that was it." Loper closed the chicken house door and glanced around. He looked very serious. "Hank! Come here!"

A cold shiver went down my spine. Yipes, they had put out a warrant for my arrest. Would I step out into the glare of the searchlights and take my punishment? That would have been the honorable course of action, the brave and noble thing to do. I had always wanted to be brave and noble, right? So . . .

I Resign
in Disgrace

I didn't move. Why? Well, because . . . hey look, I hadn't actually done anything wrong. The worst crime they could come up with was that I had been caught in the chicken house. A dog has to be somewhere, right? If I hadn't been in the chicken house, I would have been somewhere else and if I'd been somewhere else, I might have done something really bad.

Do you see where the Path of Logic has taken us? It has given its pure and simple verdict: I had gone into the chicken house to avoid being somewhere even worse. Hencely, since no crime had actually occurred, I had done exactly the right thing.

Could I explain this to Loper through tail wags

and facial expressions? Not likely, and he wouldn't accept it anyway. You know these people, always suspicious and thinking the worst of their dogs. They just don't understand. Maybe they never will.

So I'm sure you'll agree that my best course of action was to lay low and keep mum, and you'll be proud to know that I did. You'll be even prouder to know that I moved deeper into the darkness of the machine shed, turned my back on the scene outside, and covered my ears with my paws, sparing myself the, uh, tension and so forth of being screeched at.

No ordinary dog could have resolved this awkward situation with such wisdom and grace. Just look at the bottom line: no chickens had been harmed, no blood had been spilled, and I didn't have to listen to a small-minded rancher fuming and bellowing.

I guess Loper finally decided that he looked ridiculous, standing out there in his bathrobe and yelling insults at an innocent dog. When I uncovered my ears fifteen minutes later, he and Alfred had gone back inside. I crept to the crack between the big sliding doors and peered outside. Nothing remained of the ugly incident but the scars and memories.

Oh yes, it had left scars on my Inner Bean. I mean, we dogs have feelings too, tender emotions that are as fragile as the petals of a flower, and when we're accused of terrible crimes and get yelled at by the people we've tried so hard to please . . . I don't know, it causes damage. Sometimes we can bounce back and sometimes we can't.

You know what hurt the most? I had offered the olive pit of friendship to Pete, and he had stabbed me in the back and left me for crow bait. What a louse! What a bum!

As I've said many times before, never trust a cat. Too bad I can't take my own advice, but the reason is that I'm too tender-hearted and trusting. I keep hoping that the little snot will reform and become an honest citizen of the ranch, but he keeps breaking my heart.

Pretty sad, huh? I agree.

Oh, one last thing about Pete and then we'll go on to a more cheerful topic. If he hadn't offered to help on that chicken house deal, I never would have gone through with it. Honest. I'm pretty sure that I never would have attempted it on my own, so you'll be glad to know that at least half the blame must fall upon Pete.

Or to come at it from a different angle, he had

been the cause of the WHOLE SHAMEFUL INCI-
DENT. I'm sure you'll agree. Thanks.

Well, I was in the midst of these deep and
heavy thoughts when a voice in the dark scared
the living bejeebers out of me. "Oh, hi. What are
you doing in here?"

I'm sorry to report that my mind just cratered,
collapsed. I mean, all the tension of the evening
sent my circuits into Overload. I saw colored
checkers and circles of butterflies, then a folks
came into fracas . . . a face came into focus, let us
say. The face wore a silly grin and after a moment, I realized that I was staring into the eyes
of . . . "Drover? Is that you?"

"Yeah. I didn't mean to scare you."

"You didn't scare me. On your best day, you
couldn't scare a flea on a grandpa's knee."

"How come your eyeballs are rolling around?"

"My eyeballs aren't . . . where am I?"

"Well, I think we're in the machine shed."

"Yes, of course. It's all coming back. I was riding on a tour bus and . . ." I looked closer at the
face before me. "You're Drover, right?"

"Yeah, that's me, just plain old Drover."

I paced a few feet away and tried to clear the
smoke and mirrors from my mind. "Drover, we
seem to be inside the machine shed."

"Yeah, I know."

"What are we doing here?"

"Do you really want to know?"

"Of course I want to know!"

There was a moment of throbbing silence. "Well, I think you got caught in the chicken house."

Those words went through me like a wooden nickel and suddenly the memories came crashing down upon my head. I felt weak and faint. I tottered a few steps away and collapsed on the floor. "You're right. I know you're right, but why did you have to tell me at a time like this?"

"Well, 'cause you asked at a time like this . . . I guess."

"I didn't know what I was asking. I'd almost forgotten the whole shabby episode. Now you've brought it up again and . . ." I staggered to my feet. "Drover, I'm ruined, and you know what really hurts? Loper thinks I went in there to eat one of Sally May's chickens. It breaks my heart."

"Yeah, but it's true."

I glared at the runt. "Drover, I didn't eat a chicken. They can't hang me for a crime I didn't commit."

"Want to bet?"

"What?"

"I said . . . boy, this is sad."

"It's worse than sad, Drover, it's a complete disaster. By morning, the news will be all over the ranch. They'll be calling for my resignation. My reputation will be in shambles."

"Yeah, and it wasn't too great to begin with."

"Good point. I mean, my relationship with Sally May has been pretty shaky, and this . . . this will push it over the edge. She'll never believe that her own precious kitty was the cause of the entire incident."

"Pete was?" His mouth bloomed into a silly grin.

"Why are you grinning?"

"Oh nothing. I saw Pete a while ago and he was laughing his head off. He laughed so hard, he fell out of the tree."

"Good. I hope he broke his cheating little neck." I glanced around the shed. "Well, I have only one course of action left."

"Yeah, let's beat him up."

"It's not that simple, Drover. Beating up the cat would be fun, but it would solve nothing. This crisis has gotten completely out of control."

"Gosh, you mean . . ."

"Yes. I must resign my position as Head of Ranch Security and Fire Safety, and leave the ranch in disgrace. They don't want me anymore, Drover, so I must leave."

He blinked his eyes in disbelief. "Yeah, but who'll run the ranch?"

"I don't know. You, Pete, someone. I've tried to solve everyone's problems, but this one is out of my hands."

I watched as he collapsed on the cement floor, kicked all four legs, and moaned. "Help, murder, mayday! Oh, my leg! You can't do this to me!"

The prospect that he might have to grow up and do something constructive had sent him into convulsions. He was a funny little mutt. I would miss him.

I stepped over his potsrate body and walked outside. The moon and stars had vanished behind a curtain of clouds and a restless wind had begun to moan out of the northwest. Flashes of dry lightning twinkled behind the clouds.

Drover dragged himself out the door. "Will you ever come back?"

"We don't have an answer to that, son. I'll go into lonely exile and become a dog without a home. If, at some future date, the people around here realize they've made a dreadful mistake, maybe I'll return. But don't count on that." I gave

him one last pat on the shoulder. "Try to be strong. Good-bye."

Before either of us could break down in tears, I rushed out into the gloomy darkness of the dark and gloomy night. Pretty sad, huh? You bet. I mean, this was the ranch I had loved and protected and given the best years of my life, and now . . . the happy days were gone forever: sleeping beside the stove at Slim's house, fishing with Little Alfred, barking at the mailman, waiting at the yard gate for Scrap Time.

I'd lost it all . . . over a bunch of brainless chickens! It wasn't fair. I mean, a guy goes through years and years without ever thinking of chicken dinners, and then one day, for just a few fevered hours, he can't get it out of his mind and . . . poof! It's all gone, all the good decisions, all the courageous actions, all the awards and medals and citations for meriticular service . . . meritorial . . . metatarsal . . . meteorological . . .

Phooey. Years of brave and loyal service go down the sewer, and nobody remembers all the days that he watched plump chickens parading around and he didn't try to eat them.

It never should have happened, but it did. And you know what else?

It was my own fault.

There, I've said it! I hate admitting a mistake but this time I can't avoid it. I'd had the best job in the whole country and I'd blown it away. How dumb can a dog be? Pretty dumb.

With Drover's moans and sniffles in my ears, I turned toward the canyons north of ranch head-quarters and walked away from everything that was dear to me. I didn't dare to stop or look back. Overhead, lightning crackled in ugly gray clouds, but I hardly noticed.

I must have walked a couple of miles when I came to the top of a small hill. There, I stopped to rest and, well, to cast one last look at the ranch I had loved so . . . holy smokes, I suddenly realized that I wasn't alone on that hill! Peering into the darkness, I saw the vague outlines of two . . . *somethings*.

Needles of fear pricked the back of my neck and I heard a gasp of air rushing into my chest. Things had just gone from worse to awful. Can you guess who that might have been? Think of the two guys in the whole world that you would never want to meet in the dead of night.

Yes, unless I was badly mistaken, I had just blundered into a dangerous and deadly encounter with the notorious cannibal brothers, Rip and Snort.

Strangers
in the Night

My mouth had become as dry as a dirty sock
and I wasn't sure I could speak, yet I had to
say something. Let's face it. With Rip and Snort, a
guy had no chance of fighting his way out of a
mess, or even running away. They were tougher
than boot leather, faster than greased lightning,
and they had no sense of humor. None.

Could I talk my way out of this deal? I had to
try. I didn't have time to prepare one of my better
speeches, but I had to say something. I swallowed
the lump in my throat and launched into my
presentation.

"Evening, guys. Hey, this is my lucky night,
running into you two, huh?" No response. "Okay,

I can guess what you're thinking. You probably think it was pretty foolish of me to leave ranch headquarters in the middle of the night. Am I getting close?"

Not a sound, not even a grunt to acknowledge my presence. Well, that wasn't exactly a surprise. I mean, Rip and Snort weren't famous for their social skills. I plunged on.

"Not talking? That's fine, no problem. I'll do the talking and you guys can just listen, and we'll all come away from the experience . . . uh . . . with a deeper understanding of our . . . okay, about me being out here, alone and unprotected, I agree: from a certain perspective, it appears to be a reckless course of action. We all agree on that, right?"

Not a word.

"So that leaves us with what may turn out to be the . . . the most puzzling question of the entire week: gosh, why would a smart dog like me venture out into the pasture in the dark of night, and why would he walk right into the middle of a couple of possibly unfriendly coyotes?

"Ha ha. Actually, we have two questions there, not just one, and, well, that means we'll be looking for two answers, right? I mean, every question needs an answer, right? Ha ha." Silence. "Okay, guys, may I speak frankly here? Your silence is causing me a certain amount of . . . how shall I say this? Your silence is making me nervous. I'm trying my very best to answer all your questions, but I must tell you that it's hard when you just sit there like a couple of rocks."

At last a harsh hacksaw voice cut through the silence. "Junior, will you tell that dog to shut his big yap? A guy can't hardly think with him running his mouth, much less take care of his business."

Then, another voice said, "Uh-uh, okay, P-pa. H-h-hi, d-d-doggie. My p-pa w-wonders if y-you'd m-m-mind h-h-holding down the n-n-noise a l-little bit, little bit."

I almost fainted with relief. Do you see the meaning of this? Those voices hadn't come from Rip and Snort, but from a couple of buzzards named Wallace and Junior!

Holy smokes, what a piece of good luck! I mean, hanging out with buzzards can damage your reputation, but on a dark night in the wilderness, I'll take buzzards every time over a couple of hungry cannibals.

This discovery left me feeling so relieved, I ran to the buzzards, threw my arms around the smaller of the two, and pulled him into a warm

embrace. "Wallace, I never thought I'd be glad to see you again but, by George, you've made my heart sing tonight."

He fought against my hug and pushed me away. "Hyah, get away from me, unhand me, dog! If your heart wants to sing, take it somewheres else and leave the rest of us alone!"

"Well, gee whiz, I was just trying to be friendly."

"Oh yeah? Well, be friendly to somebody who wants it, and that ain't me." He smoothed down his ruffled feathers and waddled a few steps away.

I turned to Junior. "What's eating him?"

"Oh, that's j-j-just P-p-pa. H-he gets c-c-cranky s-sometimes."

Wallace yelled, "Yes, and tell him why, son. Tell him about how our business is down thirty percent this month and we ain't had enough grub to keep a grasshopper alive. An empty stomach maketh the heart grow cranky, dog, and if that don't suit you, then go back to wherever you came from and sit on a tack!"

Junior grinned and shrugged. "Th-th-that's my p-pa."

"Junior, I don't know how you can stand to be around him all the time. I'd find it a little depressing after a while."

"Oh, w-w-well he t-t-takes l-long n-naps."

"That would help, I guess."

Wallace stormed over to us and stuck his beak in my face. "And I'll tell you something else, puppy dog. Me and Junior are on Fire Patrol tonight and the last thing we need is to have some jughead dog hanging around and trying to make idle talk." He jerked his head toward Junior. "Son, get back on duty, I need to rest my eyes." He whirled back to me. "We're busy, so run along. Come back when you can't stay so long."

"Buzzards on Fire Patrol? For your information, pal, I'm the Head of Fire—" I stopped talking when I remembered that I had resigned from my post.

"Yes sir, Fire Patrol. Me and Junior have started the Buzzard Volunteer Fire Patrol and we're a-watching for fires in the night. See all that lightning over yonder? If any one of them forks of lightning was to hit the ground, we'd have ourselves a prairie fire, is what we'd have."

This was pretty funny but I tried not to laugh. "Let me get this straight. You're keeping the lightning from starting a fire?"

Wallace puffed himself up. "That's right, mister. See, I'm the fire chief around here and I've put out the word: no fires allowed while I'm on duty."

"No kidding? So you just . . . what? Talk to the lightning?"

"That's right. With this lightning, you have to lay down the law. It ain't a job for the faint of heart, I can tell you that. Watch this." Wallace turned toward the northwest where flashes of lightning were coming closer. "Listen up, all you lightnings up yonder! This here is Wallace Q. Buzzard, chief of the Fire Patrol. Y'all can twinkle and flash and play around all you want, as long as you stay up in them clouds, but the first rannihan that tries to strike the ground is going to be in a world of hurt!" He turned back to me with a smirk. "What do you say now, pooch?"

"That's very impressive, and it seems to be working."

Wallace draped a wing on my shoulder. "Puppy, let me tell you something. There ain't many creatures on this Earth that want to mess with a buzzard, and that goes double for bolts of lightning. They know what happens when a buzzard gets mad. Do *you* know what a buzzard does when he gets mad?"

"Uh . . . let me guess. He throws up on whoever made him mad?"

"That's it, yes, and we ain't talking about rosebuds and apple pie. We're talking about . . ."

"Right. I've seen some of your work and I'd rather not discuss it."

He patted my shoulder. "Good, good. Then we're on the same page, as they say, and you can probably guess what's fixing to land right on top of your head if you don't buzz off and leave me and Junior alone."

I backed away from him. "You know, Wallace, this has been fun, but I really need to be moving along."

"It ain't that we're being unfriendly, we just have things to—"

He didn't have a chance to finish his sentence. Suddenly we were blinded by a brilliant flash of lightning, followed seconds later by a blast of thunder. BOOM! It shook the earth and knocked Wallace to the ground.

"Help! Junior, they're shooting back at us, son! Don't just stand there like a goose, do something!"

It took a moment for my eyes to recover from the flash, and when they did, I found myself staring at . . . "Hey Wallace, you said you were out here scouting for fires? Well, look right in front of you."

Wallace picked himself up off the ground and peered into the darkness—darkness that had begun to show a flicker of yellow light about five feet from where Wallace was standing. "That ain't a fire."

"It is a fire, and it's getting bigger by the second."

"It ain't a fire, dog, 'cause if it was a fire, I would have seen it first. You know why?" He tapped himself on the chest. "Because the fire chief always finds the fires."

"P-p-pa?"

Wallace whirled around to Junior. "What!"

"I think h-h-he's r-r-right. It's a f-f-f-fire, a fire."

Wallace craned his neck and squinted at the flames. "Junior, you know that lightning bolt that pret' near fried us all?"

"Y-y-yeah."

"Son, it has started a fire and I'm turning in the first report. What do you reckon we ought to do?"

"Oh, m-maybe you'd b-b-better p-put it out."

"Me? Junior, the last time I tried stomping out a fire, it sure did blister the bottoms of my feet. How about you handle this one?"

"F-f-forget th-that."

Wallace whirled around to me. "Shep, how'd you like to join the fire department? We've never hired a dog before, but we're a little short-handed right now, is what we are, and there's a good job just a-waiting for the right dog."

"No thanks."

While the flames reached higher and higher, Wallace jerked his head toward Junior and back to me. "Well, I've never seen such a bunch of gold-bricking, half-stepping, yellow-bellied chicken livers! If y'all don't get yourselves out there and stomp out that fire . . ."

Just then, the wind picked up and fanned the flames into a pillar of fire that set Wallace's tail feathers ablaze. He jumped straight up in the air and started running in circles, slapping at the fire with his wings.

"Hyah, fire, hyah! Junior, don't just stand there gawking like an I-don't-know-what! Jump in here and do something!"

"P-p-pa, s-s-sit d-down!"

"Dummy! I ain't going to sit down, that's where the fire's at!"

Junior turned to me with a weary expression. "D-d-doggie, y-you t-tell him. H-h-he n-never listens to m-me."

I turned to Wallace and yelled, "Listen, birdbrain, if you'll sit on the fire, you'll put it out!"

Wallace stopped in his tracks, stared at me,

and sat down. Moments later, he stood up and studied his smoking tail section. "Well, you didn't need to screech and call names. Buzzards are pretty sensitive, down deep."

I tried not to laugh. "Sorry, Wallace."

"No, you ain't. You ain't sorry at all. I seen that grin on your face. You thought it was funny, but let me tell you something, puppy dog." He stopped talking and stepped away from the burning grass at his feet. "Junior, that fire is fixing to get out of hand."

"Y-yeah. You r-r-reckon we b-b-better p-p-put it out, put it out?"

"Put it out? Son, I'm taking early retirement and it's time to get airborne." He jerked his head back to me. "We'll leave this one for you, Shep, but try to remember this." He moved closer and whispered in my ear. "It takes only one fire to make a hot dog. Hee hee!" He yelled out to Junior. "Come on, son, last one in the air's a rotten egg!"

Wallace spread his wings, trotted into the breeze, and flapped off into the night. Junior gave me a grin and waved his wing. "I g-guess he's d-d-done playing f-f-fire chief. B-b-bye, d-doggie, and b-be c-careful."

"See you around, Junior."

I smiled to myself as I watched him fly away.

They were quite a pair, those two, and seeing Wallace's tail on fire had kind of raised my spirits. But I didn't have long to think about that because, just then, the wind made a sudden shift and began blowing hard out of the north.

I guess you know what strong wind does to a fire. In dry weather, it will turn a little fire into a roaring monster and that's just what I saw in front of me, a roaring, leaping, hissing monster of a prairie fire that sent a spray of sparks shooting up into the dark sky.

Fellers, if you've never seen a prairie fire up close, you can't understand how scary it is. It touches something deep inside a dog and makes him want to do just one thing: get as far away as possible and run for his life! It's the natural, normal response and I'm not ashamed to say that I . . . well, turned and ran like a striped ape.

Lost in
the Smoke

After I had put two hundred yards of pasture between me and the awful hissing prairie fire, only then did I dare to stop and look back. I had reached the upwind side, so I was no longer in any danger, but then I noticed . . .

HUH?

Holy tamales, the fire was moving on a course that would take it straight to the ranch house! And a voice inside my head was saying things I didn't want to hear, such as, "That thing could burn down the house! What kind of rat would walk off and leave his friends at a time like this?"

It was a pretty good question, but I had already answered it: this wasn't my problem and besides . . . well, big prairie fires are really scary.

Running from a fire was the normal thing to do, and I could find nothing shameful or disgraceful about . . .

But you know what? It WAS disgraceful! Maybe my people didn't deserve my help, but cowdogs don't just cut and run when things get tough. Ordinary mutts might do that, but not cowdogs.

I studied the eerie red glow on the clouds above the fire. Gulp. In thirty minutes or less, the fire would sweep across the pasture and flames would be leaping around the house. I didn't have a moment to lose . . . or to think about it.

Before I knew it, I had pushed the throttle all the way to Turbo Five and was racing south across the pasture. To reach the house, I would have to run around the east edge of the fire and then put myself in the very path the blaze was following. Could I do it? Yes, because I had to.

On and on I raced. Three hundred yards from the house, I checked instruments and was pleased to see that all systems looked good. I was on a straight course that would take me directly to the house, and then I would . . .

Uh-oh. You know what happens when you get downwind from a prairie fire? You're right in its path, see, and that's where all the smoke goes, downwind. I didn't happen to think of that and it

came as a nasty surprise when I found myself . . .
arg, gasp . . . lost in a choking cloud of smoke.

I mean, one second I could see the house up
ahead, and the next I could hardly even see the
end of my nose! I was surrounded on all sides by
red-glowing billows of smoke and somewhere in
the distance I could hear that awful roaring
sound.

I stopped. I had lost all sense of direction and
I could hardly breathe! Was this how it would
end, with me stumbling around in a cloud of
smoke, unable to warn my people of the danger
that was heading their way? Yes, it appeared that
my life would end in failure.

Gasping and choking, I sank to the ground.
The roar of the fire filled my ears as it moved
closer, ever closer. Strength ebbed out of my body.
I had nothing left. I melted into the grass, rolled
over, and took one last look at . . .

Huh? Buzzards? Was I dreaming or had the
smoke parted for just a second and allowed me to
catch a glimpse of two buzzards flapping overhead? In a flash, the vision was gone, swallowed
up by a swirl of smoke and sparks.

It must have been a dream, perhaps my last. I
couldn't resist a bitter laugh at such a cruel fate,
that one of my last thoughts on this Earth had

been about buzzards. I closed my eyes and waited for the drama to play itself out. But then . . .

"Pooch, you can lay there like a dead log if you want, but if it was me, I'd get up and run!"

I opened my eyes just in time to catch a glimpse of a big black bird swooping through the smoke, and then he was gone. I lifted my head and blinked my stinging eyes against the smoke. "Wallace? Is that you?"

A voice came out of the smoke above my head. "Heck yes, it's me, and I ain't just flapping around for my health! Do you want me and Junior to lead you out of this fire or would you rather lay there and get roasted?"

I struggled to my feet and gasped for air. "I'll choose number one, but I can't see you in all this smoke!"

"Well, dog, I can't do a thing about the smoke, so try to follow the sound of my voice! Reckon you can do that? I mean, I ain't going to take you by the hand and lead you out of there. Me and Junior are going to *sing* you out of the fire."

"What? You're going to *sing,* is that what you said?"

"Yes sir. This is Junior's big idea, not mine, and you can either follow the sound of our voices or sit there and fry!"

Hmm. Okay, I was about to be sung out of a crisis by a couple of buzzards. That struck me as pretty strange, but I didn't have any better ideas. I still couldn't see them through all the smoke, but a moment later, I heard them strike up a song. Musically speaking, it wasn't all that great, but don't forget, they were only buzzards. A guy doesn't expect great music to come from the mouths of buzzards.

Call in the Dogs, Put Out the Fire
Dark night, summertime, dry as a bone.
Call in the dogs, put out the fire.
South wind moans like a saxophone.
Call in the dogs, put out the fire.

Dry grass waiting like gasoline.
Call in the dogs, put out the fire.
One little spark . . . it could sure be mean.
Call in the dogs, put out the fire.

Old Shep's a faithful dog, all right.
Call in the dogs, put out the fire.
He sleeps all day and barks all night.
Call in the dogs, put out the fire.

Old Shep stands guard at the chicken pen.
Call in the dogs, put out the fire.
He eats him one every now and then.
Call in the dogs, put out the fire.

Here, Shep, you better come home!
This ain't the night for you to roam.
Old Shep, you've barked the whole night
through.
You'd better come home, I'm a-telling you.

Shep barks at thunder, mean and loud.
Call in the dogs, put out the fire.
He ain't a-scared of a thunder cloud.
Call in the dogs, put out the fire.

Shep barks at lightning just for fun.
Call in the dogs, put out the fire.
One of these days, gonna catch him one.
Call in the dogs, put out the fire.

Watch out, Old Shep, that lightning struck!
Call in the dogs, put out the fire.
Prairie fire rolls like a ten-ton truck!
Call in the dogs, put out the fire.

That fire, it's roaring like a mob.
Call in the dogs, put out the fire.
Old Shep, you didn't do your job.
Call in the dogs, put out the fire.

Shep, Shep, you better come home!
This ain't the night for you to roam.
Old Shep, you've barked the whole night
    through.
How'd you like to be barbecue?

Call in the dogs, put out the fire.
Call in the dogs, put out the fire.

Well, what can you say about that? As buzzard
music, I guess it wasn't too bad and it did get me
through the smoke and out of the fire, but other
than that . . . well, it wasn't a great work of art.

So, yes, I stumbled and staggered through the
cloud of smoke, following the sound of the Singing
Buzzards, and not for one second did I ever know
where I was. This was what you'd call Blind Faith
in action. Then, all at once, I popped out of the
cloud and found myself about fifty yards north of
the machine shed. Overhead, Wallace and Junior
were floating around in the updrafts.

I yelled, "Well, thanks for the help, guys. I'll sure remember this."

Wallace yelled back, "You do that, pooch. Next time, maybe we'll have you for supper, if you get my meaning. Hee!"

"I get your meaning, but don't hold your breath. It takes more than one little prairie fire to bring me down."

"Yeah, we noticed. If it hadn't been for me and Junior, you'd be charcoal. Now let's see if you can put out the fire, pooch."

"Yeah? Well, you watch, 'cause that's what I'm fixing to do."

I sprinted down to the yard. At the fence, I paused a moment, wondering if I dared to enter Sally May's yard. Yes, surely she would want to know that her house and home were about to be torched to the ground, if someone didn't do something in a big hurry.

I coiled my legs under me, leaped upward and outward, and landed inside Sally May's yard. There, I sprinted toward the back porch and was about to launch my Warning Barks, when I saw . . . hmmm . . . a cat was sitting in the middle of the porch, with his tail wrapped around his body. Oh, and he was smirking.

"Well, well!" said Pete. "I wondered how long it would take you to notice the fire."

"Oh yeah? Did you wonder how I got trapped in the chicken house?"

"Actually, Hankie, I didn't wonder about that." He fluttered his eyelashes. "I had inside information, you know. Tee hee. You certainly got everyone stirred up."

"That's right, kitty, and I'm fixing to stir *you* up."

"Now, now, don't be bitter."

"And by the way, Pete, if you saw the fire, why didn't you sound the alarm, huh?"

He gave that some thought. "You know, Hankie, I did think about it, but, well, cats don't do that."

"So you were just going to sit here and let the fire burn down the whole ranch?"

"Well, Hankie, we cats always seem to land on our feet"—he flashed an insolent smirk—"no matter what happens to everyone else."

"Oh yeah? We'll see about that!"

In a flash, I snatched him up by the scruff of his neck and pitched him as far I could throw him. Heh heh. I'll give you a hint: he didn't land on his feet. He crashed headfirst into the fence. I paused a moment to enjoy his hissing and yowling, but had to return to the urgent mission that had brought me there.

I took a huge gulp of air and began the program we call Alert and Alarm. As you may remember, this consists of blast after blast of Urgency Barks. These are not the same barks we use on cats, coyotes, or skunks, but rather barks that are shrill and passionate, so loaded with emotion that nobody inside the house can possibly ignore them.

I fired off round after round of Urgencies, barked myself down to skin and bones, and almost passed out from lack of oxygen. But to my complete amazement, nobody answered the call.

I couldn't believe this! What did it take? I dashed around to the north side of the house and took up a position right under Loper and Sally May's bedroom window. This time, they couldn't ignore me. I reloaded my tanks with air and resumed barking. The window was open, and with only a screen between me and them, I was sure they would hear me.

"May I have your attention please? This is a news bulletin from the ranch's Security Division. We have a monster prairie fire approaching headquarters, and if you'll pardon me for saying so, Loper, you might want to get out of bed and grab a bucket of—"

"Hank, shut up that barking!"

"Water, and no, I will not shut up my barking, meathead, because—"

"HUSH UP!"

See what I have to put up with? A dog barks his heart out and tries to warn his people, and what good does it do? They never listen to their dogs, but this time they were going to listen, like it or not.

I had some serious reservations about diving through the window, but they had left me no choice. Before I could think about the hazards of jumping through a window screen, I entered all the targeting information into Data Control's mainframe computer. When the Launch Button flashed on the console of my mind, I coiled my leg muscles and fired the weapon.

CRASH!

Was I cut to ribbons by the window screen? Did I live long enough to wake up my people or did we all burn up in the awful fire? To find out, you'll just have to keep on reading.

I Take Charge

Boy, you talk about sounds that will bring a sleeping rancher out of his bed! When I went ripping through the window screen, that did it! Loper sat straight up and muttered, "What the Sam Hill!" There was a moment of eerie silence, then I heard him jump out of bed and stumble over to the window. "Sally May, wake up, hon, we've got a fire coming this way!"

Well, glory be! But you see what I had to do to get his attention? Oh, and do you suppose anybody bothered to check my body for cuts and wounds? No sir. Lucky for me, I had come through the ordeal without a scratch, but still . . . oh well.

Loper turned on the light and suddenly the

place became a beehive of action. While Sally May flew out of bed and slipped into her bathrobe, Loper scrambled into his clothes and ran for the telephone in the kitchen. He dialed a number and paced while it rang.

"Slim? Loper. Big fire in the home pasture. Start calling the neighbors. Call the fire department, then get up here as quick as you can." He leaned over so that he could see the fire through the utility room window. "Slim, tell 'em we need heavy equipment. We won't stop this one with a water truck. Hurry!"

Loper hung up the phone and walked out into the utility room. For several moments, he stared through the window at the red monster that lit up the night sky. His shoulders sagged and his head slumped forward.

Sally May joined him. She gazed out the window and let out a gasp. "Oh my heavens, it's huge!"

He put his arm around her shoulder. "Hon, we'll fight this thing as best we can, but there's a chance that we might lose the house. I'm going to start hosing down the shingles. They're wood and they'll be the first things to burn. Wake up the kids and load the car with anything you want to save."

For a moment, she seemed too shocked to speak. "Save? What do you save from a whole lifetime?"

"Not much, but that's where we are. I want you and the kids to get out of here right away. Go down to Viola's place and wait until I call."

"And you?"

"Slim's calling the neighbors and the fire department. We'll give it our best shot."

Their eyes met and she said, "I'll stay here and help . . . at least for a while."

"Hon . . ."

"If it looks hopeless, we'll leave."

He gave her a kiss on the cheek. "All right, old gal, let's get moving." They turned and started toward the kitchen. I had been sitting there, watching, and all at once I felt very uneasy about . . . well, being inside Sally May's house. You know how she is: no dogs in the house, ever.

Not only was I inside her house, but I had wrecked the screen on her bedroom window to get there. Gulp.

I lowered my head and began tapping out a slow rhythm with my tail. *Tap, tap, tap.* When she saw me, her face went toxic right away, but then it softened. She paused long enough to give me two pats on the back and said, "Thanks, Hank. You were very brave."

Wow! Did you hear that? She said I was brave! I was so moved by her words, I wilted to the floor, rolled over on my back, and waited for the flurry of pats and rubs that I so richly deserved.

Huh?

Okay, they hurried out of the room and began their preparations. That was all right. I understood. After all, we had a fire bearing down on us and I could wait for my pats and rubs.

Whilst Sally May woke up the children, Loper grabbed his hat and left through the back door. I went with him. If there was a fire to fight, I wanted to be right in the middle of it, doing my part and showing the flag of the Security Division.

And besides, I had no great desire to stay in the house with Sally May. I mean, she had called me a brave dog, but don't forget that unfortunate incident in the chicken house. She would have heard about it and she had a long memory. A guy never wants to push his luck.

Outside in the yard, we could hear the distant crackle of the fire and saw the rise and fall of the red glow behind the curtain of smoke. Loper didn't say anything, but I could guess his thoughts. That thing was really scary. It made a grown man feel about the size of an ant, and a grown dog, too.

But there was a bit of good news. The wind had slacked up and the fire line had slowed its march toward the house. That gave us a little time to prepare a defense.

Loper turned on the water hose and sprayed the roof. After about five minutes, we looked off to the northeast and saw several pairs of headlights coming down the county road. Hooray, we had reinforcements!

The first to arrive was Slim, followed by Billy and several other ranch neighbors from down the creek. They had come prepared to fight fire with shovels and wet gunnysacks. I had a feeling that wouldn't be enough. Where was that "heavy equipment" Loper had mentioned on the phone?

When Alfred came out of the house, Loper gave him the water hose and let him finish the job of wetting down the roof.

Loper gathered the crew together. "All right, boys, with a fire this big, the best we can do is save the house. There's no way we can put it out. We'll move out into the pasture about a hundred yards and start a backfire. Let's go."

In case you're not familiar with some of the technical terms we use in the firefighting business, let me explain "backfire." You probably thought a backfire was something an old pickup does when you let off the gas pedal. Well, that's one of its meanings, but in the firefighting business, we have something else in mind.

See, we burn a narrow strip of pasture that lies in the path of a prairie fire, the idea being that when the big fire gets there, it won't have any fuel. It's called a fireguard.

But the most important part of any backfire procedure is the presence of a well-trained, experienced, fearless cowdog who will race up and down the line, delivering blast after blast of stern Anti-Fire Barking. You can have the best fireguard in the world, but if you don't have that dog doing his stuff, well, you might as well be blowing soap bubbles. Nothing works.

I'm not saying that a crew of men doesn't help, but they're mainly just a backup for the dog. Without that dog, fellers, the whole business just seems to fall apart. No kidding.

Anyway, I sent my men out into the pasture to backfire a strip of grass and prepare the fireguard. While they worked, I watched them closely because . . . well, let's face it. When you have to depend on guys like Slim Chance to finish a job, you can't relax. The man was a goof-off, a cowboy joker who had caught his own pants on fire that very afternoon, and I had to watch him like a clock.

Hawk. I had to hawk him like a clock.

I had to clock him like a . . .

I supervised the whole backfiring operation, is the point, and my crew did a pretty good job, all things considered, and at that moment there wasn't much we could do but wait for the fire to arrive. That was a little creepy, standing there in what should have been black darkness and watching this glowing, roaring, crackling THING moving toward us.

We watched and waited. The wind had died to a whisper and the atmosphere was strangely calm except for the crackle of the fire. The men leaned on their shovels and talked in low voices, their faces smudged with soot and lit by the glow of the approaching flames. Now and then one of them would laugh. They seemed pretty confident that we would stop the fire. I wasn't so sure.

Sally May and the children came out to join us and brought a jug of drinking water for the men. I was watching them drink (had anyone offered ME some water? No), when Little Alfred came up behind me and put his arm around my neck.

He leaned down to my ear and whispered, "Hankie, what were you doing in the chicken house?"

Huh? The chicken house? Why were we bringing up ancient history?

"Mom thinks you were going to eat one of her hens."

I whapped my tail on the ground and gave the boy a look of greatest sincerity. "Fire safety. I was, uh, giving your mother's chickens a class on fire safety . . . you know, what to do in the event of a fire emergency. Son, there's no substitute for training."

I was in the process of studying the boy's face when we were blasted by a sudden gust of cold wind, the leading edge of a thunderstorm. All eyes turned to the north and what we saw sent chills of terror down every spine. Two hundred yards to the north, the monster had been awakened. Red and yellow claws of flame leaped into the air . . . hissing, popping, roaring, throwing showers of red sparks high into the night sky . . . and the thing was racing toward us again!

I felt a powerful urge to run, shall we say, but Alfred tightened his grip around my neck as he stared at the fire with wide eyes. So I held my position. I mean, what kind of dog would run off and leave his pal behind?

The men shielded their faces from the heat and sparks, and shrank back toward the house. Loper yelled, "Sally May, load the kids in the car and get out of here, while you still can!"

Sally May scooped up the baby, then took Alfred's hand and ran for the car, which was parked behind the house. Naturally, I went with them, I mean, what could be more important than guarding Sally May and her children? They would need an escort to lead them through the smoke and confusion, right? Of course they would.

When we reached the car, she jerked open the back door and told Alfred to jump inside. I was almost sure that she called my name too, so I vaulted up into the backseat and . . .

"Hank, not you!"

. . . and pressed myself against Alfred's body. A boy and his dog. Surely she wouldn't . . .

She leaned into the car. "Hank, you're covered with soot. Stay here with the men. Maybe you can help . . . or something."

Hmmm. Good point. The Head of Ranch Security needed to stay at the front. I turned to my little pal.

"Son, take care of your ma. I can't leave this fire until we have it licked." And to add emphasis to my remarks, I gave him a juicy lick on the cheek and dived out of the car. Sally May closed the door and they sped off into the night.

All Is Lost!

Well, I had made a successful evacuation of the women and children, and now it was time to . . .

Yipes! Suddenly, the roar of the fire filled my ears. The blaze had reached the fireguard, and sparks and firebrands were raining down on the roof of the house, in the yard, everywhere! Loper grabbed the water hose and sprayed the fires on the roof, while Slim and the others beat out fires in the yard with shovels and wet gunnysacks.

So far, so good. Every eye turned back to the north, watching to see if the fireguard would do its job. For a minute or two, it appeared that it would, but then the wind rose to a screaming gale and . . .

HERE IT CAME!

Like an enormous jungle cat, the thing leaped into the air and landed on the other side of the fireguard. Smoke, flames, sparks, and chunks of burning grass filled the sky. All at once the air was as hot as an oven. The wooden shingles on the roof burst into flame. The shrubs next to the house caught fire. Men yelled and gasped for air, while I . . . well, ran around in circles, barking, because, frankly, I couldn't think of anything else to do.

Then, over the noise and confusion, Loper's voice rang out. "We've lost it, boys! Run for the creek! Run for your lives!"

Well, that sure made sense to me. I mean, I had already figured out that running in circles wasn't getting us anywhere, so I pushed the throttle down to Turbo Six, and . . .

WHAM!

We've come to the sad part of the story, so grab onto something steady. In all the madness and confusion, I had somehow failed to notice . . . well, a tree, a big tree, a very large and immovable tree in the blackness of the inky darkness of the night. And in my haste to evacuate our hopeless situation, I bashed into it with a full head of steam.

I don't want to scare the children, but I have to report the facts. While the other guys on the fire team dropped their shovels and ran for their lives, the Head of Ranch Security was involved in a serious accident. And as the roar of the fire drew closer and closer, he lay wounded and unconscious . . . right in the path of the firestorm.

And, well, I guess that's about it. With me knocked out and the fire running wild toward the house, there isn't much hope for a happy ending, is there? I've always preferred happy endings to the other kind, but we don't always control the way things turn out, do we?

No. See, I'm trying to prepare you for the worst . . . but wait. There's one little detail we haven't discussed, and I'm sure it's one you never ever would have considered.

You remember that blast of cold wind that brought the fire back to life? Well, it came from a line of thunderclouds that were moving in from the northwest. Where there's lightning, there's thunder; where there's thunder, there's a thunderhead cloud; and where there's a thunderhead cloud, there could be . . . RAIN.

Fellers, it rained, and we're talking about the sky opening up and raining down snakes and weasels. Hard rain, drenching rain, fire-killing rain.

I don't know how long I lay there, knocked cuckoo, but the next thing I knew, I was lying in a puddle of water. Rain was falling in my face and a strange dog with a stub tail was standing over me. Blinking my eyes against the vapors inside my head, I looked closer and recognized . . . Drover.

He said, "Oh, good. I thought you were dead."

"I'm not dead, but it was pretty close. I got run over by a tree."

"I'll be derned. I didn't know trees could run."

"This one did. What's going on around here?"

"Well, let me think. I heard you barking at the fire and then it started raining and the fire went out."

"What!" I sat up and glanced around. It was pouring rain! And the air was filled with the smell of stale smoke, and yes, the fire was deader than a hammer! "Yes? Go on."

"I just wondered if you barked up the rain."

"Help me up, Drover." He helped me up to a standing position and I wobbled around on two pairs of shaky legs. "I'm shocked that you even needed to ask. I mean, the evidence is all here, isn't it?"

"Well, I wondered. Tell me the whole story. I can hardly wait."

"Let's see if I can remember it all. Okay, Loper and his crew did their best, but the fire rolled over them and, well, I hate to point this out, but you saw what they did. They ran for their lives."

"Yeah, and you stayed behind. Boy, what a hero!"

My legs had recovered enough so that I was able to begin pacing, as I often do when I'm trying to discuss difficult concepts. "Let's don't make too much of this, Drover. Some would call it incredible heroism, but to me, it was just another day on the job. Someone had to whip the fire and . . . well, I was the one."

His eyes sparkled in amazement. "But how'd you get it to rain?"

"It has to do with the tone of the barking, son. By making small adjustments in our standard Anti-Fire Barking Procedure, I was able to release a powerful wave of sonic energy into the clouds."

"Gosh, no fooling?"

"Yes, and, well, you see the results. It was our last hope."

"Yeah, and then you got run over by a tree."

"Exactly. Boy, what a wreck! I'm just lucky I survived."

"Yeah, and what a victory! You made it rain and put out the fire!"

I halted my pacing and looked up at the dark sky. "Actually, the experience leaves me very humble, Drover. When you find yourself in possession of such amazing powers, it . . . I find this hard to explain. Nobody can understand how it is, up here at the top of the mountain. Let me just say that I'm grateful that it worked and I feel very, very humble."

Well, that's about all the story. Was that a great ending or what? I had patched things up with Sally May, Little Alfred didn't have to spend the rest of his life living in a cardboard box, and, best of all, Pete the Barncat got soaked in the rain. Ho ho! I loved it. You should have seen the little snot: ears plastered down on his head, his tail soaked and ugly, water dripping off his chin, and mad, very mad. Hee hee.

To be honest, I'm not sure Slim and Loper ever figured out who had saved the ranch, but that's okay. When you get to be Head of Ranch Security, you take life one day at a time, knowing that your most noble and heroic deeds might go unnoticed. That's just part of being a dog.

Case . . .

Oh, by the way, don't forget why I was in the chicken house that night: *to teach fire safety to the chickens.* No kidding. Hey, I probably saved their lives, so don't believe any of those ugly rumors.

Guard dogs don't eat chickens.

Case slurped.

Closed.

Have you read all of Hank's adventures?

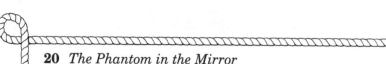